THE SCIENCE INSPECTORS

BOOK TWO

The Case of the Broken Watch

The Science Inspectors
www.bakkenbooks.com

Daniel Kenney

Edition 1
Published by Bakken Books
ISBN: 978-1-955657-74-7

www.bakkenbooks.com

Table of Contents

1. All In The Name....1
2. Pizza Plans....11
3. Not On My Watch....20
4. A Baffling Buffet....29
5. Passing The Test Tube....37
6. Recipe For Confusion....47
7. Confection Inspection....57
8. Going Rogue....66
9. Desperate Escape....75
10. Kuhl And Complicated....85
11. Honk For Rubies....95
12. Country Clubbing....109
13. Portrait Of A Crime....119
14. A Hardware Issue....130
15. A Reputation To Protect....136
16. Finally Home....145

CHAPTER 1

ALL IN THE NAME

Angela Moretti slammed her tray down so hard that some applesauce flew into the air and hit Howey Doohan smack-dab in the face. He licked his lips and smiled. "Thanks, Angela. Now I can skip seconds."

She shot him an apologetic look. "Sorry about that. I'm just annoyed."

"You don't say," Norah Sloan said sarcastically. "Jamie, could you tell that Angela was annoyed?"

Jamie McDermott took a bite of his soggy chicken sandwich and shook his head. "No way. Moretti here is a rock. The way she keeps things inside, you can't ever tell what she's thinking or how she's feeling. Our girl's a real mystery."

Howie wiped off his face. "Nope. A mystery wrapped up in a puzzle and decorated with an enigma."

Angela gave each of her friends a withering look. "You

all about done now, or does this comedy routine need more time?"

Jamie shrugged. "I think we made our point. So, why are you annoyed?"

"Correction," Norah said. "Why are you annoyed *today*?"

"First of all, in my defense, I was born this way. My mom and dad always said so. One time when I was four, I was so mad at a fly in our house that I decided to get rid of it with a baseball bat. I got that fly all right, but I also got a painful lesson in how to patch drywall. And secondly, and even more to the point, I basically live in an Italian restaurant. Being annoyed and getting angry is as natural to us as breathing."

"And because you get so agitated so quickly, you are awfully fun to tease," Norah said. "So, what's annoying you so much today?"

"Not what," Angela said. "Who. And the answer is Nina Marcus, the single worst person in the world."

Norah, Howey, and Jamie exchanged glances and then, as if on cue, they each rolled their eyes.

That fired Angela up even more. "Oh, no—you did not just roll your eyes at me."

Howey made a sympathetic face. "Listen, Angela. The thing is, we warned you. We told you Nina was the worst."

"And yet, you're still surprised," Jamie said.

"I am," Angela admitted. "It's like she's a virus. And you've all had the last several years to build up an immunity to her, but I haven't. Or rather, I'm not numb to it like the three of you. I just hate to see people who are objectively terrible get away with it over and over again."

"Trust me," Norah said, "we all do. But in case you forgot, there's a reason why Nina gets away with it."

"You're talking about her father?"

"Yes, Angela, I am. You may think Nina is the worst person in the world, but she's not. That accolade belongs to her doting dad."

"Gregori Marcus," Jamie said with a low growl.

"Just what exactly makes this guy so bad?" Angela asked.

"Exactly?" Howie said with a bit of a tremble. "I'm not sure anyone knows."

Jamie nodded. "Which is one of the reasons why he isn't behind bars. That guy is as slippery as a snake, and smart in that Chicago street-smart sort of way."

"Plus, he's ruthless," Norah said. "Intimidation and cruelty have a way of keeping lips shut, if you know what I mean. Nina is bad, but at least for now, it's the kind of bad we can all tolerate. Hurt pride. Humiliation. Not fun, but much better than a pair of broken legs."

"And you're saying that trying to teach Nina a lesson is a bad idea because of the—"

"Aforementioned broken legs," Norah said, cutting Angela off. "That's precisely what I'm saying."

Angela threw up her hands. "I just can't believe we have to let a girl like Nina Marcus act this way."

"Well, Moretti," Norah said, "until Gregori Marcus is behind bars and no longer a threat to people like you and me, that's just the way it has to be."

"I hate that."

"I know you do, Angela," Howie said. "We all hate it, but do you mind if we talked about something else? Talking about Gregori Marcus upsets my tummy, and I really want to go back and get more tater tots."

"I thought you weren't going to get seconds," Angela observed.

"On applesauce, silly. But I still plan on getting more tots, another yogurt, and two more cartons of chocolate milk."

"Howie Doohan, you are a human garbage dump."

Norah smiled. "He's more like an anaerobic digester."

Jamie and Angela exchanged blank stares. Which was all Norah needed to be... well, Norah.

"You see, an anaerobic digester is a tank or a pit

where you combine organic material and moisture and heat. And if you keep those conditions just right, over time, special bugs consume the waste and other bugs come along and consume those bugs until eventually you are left with a lot less organic material and a whole lot of something else."

"What?" Angela asked.

Norah slapped Howie on the back. "Gas. Methane gas, to be precise. Just like our Howie."

Howie smiled proudly while Jamie and Angela laughed.

"Fine," Angela finally said when the laughter died down. "No more talk about the Marcuses. What do you guys want to talk about?"

"How about the weather?" Howie said.

"The weather? What are we, a group of old folks down at the donut shop?" Jamie asked.

"I'm serious. Norah mentioned how an anaerobic digester like me needs heat. Well, trust me, I've got plenty of heat right now. Did you know that yesterday was one of the hottest October days on record here in Chicago?"

"It *was* pretty awful," Angela agreed. "The restaurant kitchen was so hot yesterday, I thought I would melt."

"Don't encourage him, Angela," Norah said. "This is

the part where Howie goes into his long diatribe about the evils of global warning. So, before he gets started, I will just say this. Yes, yesterday was hot. But last winter was one of the coldest in Chicago's history."

"Exactly," Jamie said. "And did you see that there was a huge snowstorm out east yesterday? I can't remember where exactly, but it was the earliest snowfall in that city's history. October ninth! Beating the old record by two days. I'm sure those people would love a little global warming right about now."

"Fine," Howie said. "Don't call it 'global warming.' Call it 'climate change,' for all I care. All I know is that to have the hottest October day in Chicago's history and for some city out east to have the earliest snowfall on the same day? That seems pretty crazy to me."

"It's weather," Angela said. "Isn't it always crazy and unpredictable? My mom used to say, 'If you don't like the weather, just wait a minute.'"

Norah raised her hand. "All in favor of agreeing with Howie that the weather is crazy so we can talk about something else, say aye."

Norah, Jamie, and Angela all said "aye" in unison.

Howie frowned. "Fine. What do *you* want to talk about, best friend?"

"How about the school nickname?"

Angela frowned. "The nickname? What are you talking about? I thought we were the Eagles. I finally just learned the fight song. And newsflash—it's a *terrible* fight song."

"We're the Eagles for now," Jamie explained. "But apparently some other Chicago middle school I'd never even heard of complained because they're also the Eagles, and they demanded that we change."

"Fun fact," Howie said. "'Eagles' is the most popular school nickname in America. Second fun fact—'Wildcats' is number two and 'Panthers' is number three which is funny to me because, hello, a wildcat and a panther are just about the same thing. I mean, really."

"Thank you, Howie, for that daily dose of nearly useless trivia," Norah said.

"You're most welcome."

Jamie continued. "And the school district caved, and guess what? Since Beveridge is the newer school, we are the ones who have to come up with the new nickname."

"How did I miss this drama?"

Norah smirked. "Probably the same adorable cluelessness that led you to stepping on a toilet paper bomb your first day of school."

Jamie laughed hard at that one, seeing as he was the one who had built the ingenious device. But as soon as

Angela drilled her eyes into him, he stopped.

Then, turning to the others, she added, "It's probably the fact that I'm doing everything I can to get used to a new city, a new school, and working in an Italian restaurant in all my free time. So, what's the new nickname going to be?"

"The students will vote at a school assembly on Friday."

"But I've heard about three contenders," Jamie said. "The Jackrabbits, the Bison, and... the Rubies."

"Rubies?" Angela said. "That's terrible. Who would ever want a nickname like 'Rubies'?"

Jamie, Norah, and Howie exchanged uncomfortable looks.

"What?" Angela asked. "What am I missing?"

"Word on the street is that 'Rubies' is the odds-on favorite to win," Norah said.

"How is that possible?" Angela asked.

"It's a terrible name, I'll give you that," Jamie said. "So, you've got to ask yourself—what student at this school would have the ability to convince an entire student body to vote for a terrible name?"

Angela didn't have to think long before the answer hit her like a city bus-sized migraine headache. "Oh, no."

The three of them nodded. "Oh, yes," Howie said.

"Nina Marcus wants us to be called the Rubies?"

"Apparently rubies are Nina's birthstone, she decided that's what she wanted, and so poof! It's happening," Howie explained.

Angela slumped in her chair. "She really is the worst."

"Yes, Angela, like we said before. She is. So, get used to it," Norah said.

But Angela didn't want to get used to it. As her friends continued to talk, she zoned out, nibbling on her sandwich and thinking about the unfairness in the world. A world in which people like the Marcuses were thriving and getting to do whatever they wanted. Suddenly and quite instinctively, Angela slammed her fist on the table. Luckily, there was no more applesauce to spray on Howie's face.

"No," she said defiantly.

"No, what?" Howie asked.

"No, I'm not going to get used to it. I don't believe we should just sit around and let the Nina Marcuses of the world do whatever they want, whenever they want."

"But you remember the thing we said about her father?" Jamie said.

"I do. Which means, we can't do it the Chicago street-thug way. If we're going to stop Nina, we have to be smarter. We all love science, and that means we're smart. Smarter than she is. There has to be a way for us to use our brains to stop her. Do you really want to be the Beveridge Rubies? Cuz I sure don't. So, let's find a way to stop Nina from getting what she wants. And let's be so smart about it that she doesn't even know what we did. Are you in?"

She looked around at her friends and could tell that Jamie especially was skeptical. That gave Angela a simple but brilliant idea. She leaned back in her chair. "It's kind of what I figured. You probably aren't smart enough to pull it off anyway."

Jamie narrowed his eyes. "Did you just say I wasn't smart enough?"

"To pull off something like this? Probably not."

Jamie crossed his arms and set his jaw. "I'm in. I'm just curious about what your plan is."

The bell rang, marking the end of lunch.

"Simple, really. But if we do it right, also incredibly effective. I'll explain more tonight over a slice of deep dish at Big Lou's."

"Tonight? What if I'm busy tonight?" Jamie asked.

"You won't be busy because if we're going to pull it off this week, we have no time to waste. See you tonight."

CHAPTER 2

PIZZA PLANS

Big Lou, his ample belly, and his wide smile brought over the large deep-dish pepperoni pizza just as Howie sat down.

"To my favorite kids. Enjoy!"

Big Lou walked away as Norah took out a bag with her own utensils specially sterilized for times like this. Angela took her gaze off the pizza and set it on Howie. He wasn't in his usual gray coveralls. Instead, he was wearing jeans and a green flannel shirt. The outfit looked every bit as hot and stuffy as the coveralls would on such an unusually steamy day, and Angela was curious about the change.

"What gives, Howie? I thought it was in the second-best friend contract that you had to notify me of any alterations to your regular wardrobe."

Howie grabbed his slice of pizza and took a sip of the root beer that was waiting for him. "You're right—the contract should probably have that clause in it. Trust me, I'm not happy about it. My dad insisted I wash my coveralls because he said they were starting to stink."

Norah arched an eyebrow. "Starting to?"

"Fine, he said they were starting to stink more than normal. Well, that caught me off guard because I had to find something else to wear."

"And on the hottest day we've had in a month, you decided to wear jeans and flannel?" Jamie asked. "Why didn't you just wear shorts and a T-shirt?"

"I have a rule. I only wear shorts during gym class and at the pool. So, I chose my second favorite article of clothing. My green flannel." He took a big bite of his pizza and decided that was the perfect time to keep talking. "So, what did I miss?"

"Angela is about to unveil her scheme for getting back at Nina without her knowing we're getting back at her, and if I'm right, her plan relies on a scientific principle."

"Right as usual, Norah." Angela turned to Jamie. "You were especially skeptical when I introduced the idea at lunch today. But then, I suddenly convinced you to want to try anyway. Why is that?"

Jamie scratched his chin as he thought it over. "I guess because you said I probably wasn't smart enough to pull it off."

"And that made you eager to show me that you are in fact smart enough, correct?"

"Yeah, I guess that's right."

"That's the same sort of thing we're going to do with Norah. It's a form of what's called reverse psychology."

Howie's eyes widened. "I've heard of that."

Norah held up a finger. "And it's based on a principle called psychological reactance."

Angela smiled. "Right again. I was doing some research on this after school when I was supposed to be helping out in the restaurant. Psychological reactance is the idea that something will be wanted more if people are told they can't have it. Parents use this all the time when their kids are young. At least, my dad would. 'Hey, Angela. I bet you're not strong enough to work the vacuum.' And I'd get mad about it and say I sure was. And he would doubt me and then I would go vacuum the living room just to show him. And boom—my dad got me to do a chore using reverse psychology. That's exactly what I did to you."

Jamie frowned. "I knew that."

"At the time, I'm not so sure. I think you were so busy being offended that you didn't realize I was trying to manipulate you."

"And you're saying we can do this to Nina?" Jamie asked.

"Maybe, if we're subtle and clever enough. But here's our big problem."

"Her dad?"

"No. It's Nina. You see, Jamie, she's much smarter than you are."

The four friends laughed, then ate their pizza and drank their sodas while Angela explained the basics of the plan.

"Right now, Norah wants our school to be the Beveridge Rubies, which makes me want to punch myself. I thought, as long as she wants us to have a ridiculous nickname, let's go even bigger. Let's think of something way worse and then convince her to support it using nothing other than reverse psychology."

"How exactly would we do that?" Norah asked.

Angela took a big bite and smiled a gross pizza-filled smile. "That's where you all come in. I can't do everything around here. Remember, Norah, I'm just one of your misfits. But first things first. I say we choose a nickname even more terrible than 'Rubies.'"

They brainstormed for the next ten minutes with Norah taking notes on her phone. Then they settled on a top three.

"So, our top three worst school nicknames are the Pink Ponies, the Broken Feathers, and the Strong Fighters. Do we want to vote so we can spend some time on how we're actually going to pull this off by Friday?"

"What's happening Friday?" a big booming voice asked from Angela's right. She turned to see Big Lou back at their table.

"Our school is voting on a new nickname."

Big Lou looked incredulous. "A new nickname? Beveridge Middle School has been the Eagles forever."

"I know, Big Lou," Jamie said. "But now we have to change. Don't ask us why because we don't really understand it. But if you were to come up with a new nickname, what would you choose?"

"If it were up to me? Hmm. I suppose..." He broke out into another big smile. "If it were up to me, I would call us the 'Beveridge Big Lou's Pizza.' Because that means more business for me."

That got a laugh out of the table, then Big Lou noticed Howie and looked at him curiously. "Hey, nice green flannel. Where's your usual outfit?"

Howie smiled. "I thought I'd wear something extra breathable on account of the hot weather."

Big Lou didn't catch the sarcasm, but waved his hand in front of his face. "Hot is right. Too hot for October, if you ask me."

"And if you ask me," another voice bellowed, "it's refreshing."

Big Lou turned around, as did the kids, to see a tall man amble toward them carrying a to-go box of pizza. Big Lou clapped his hands together. "Sid Granger, as I live and breathe. I didn't know you were in town."

Sid was wearing blue jeans and a bright blue Buffalo Bills T-shirt. Big Lou scowled. "You gotta lotta nerve wearing a Bills shirt in this establishment, you know that? This is Bears country."

"You seem to forget I grew up here, Big Lou. Of course it's Bears country, and of course I root for the Bears every week. I even bet on them occasionally—that is, unless they're playing my beloved Bills."

"So, just in town for a visit?"

Sid shook his head. "Had to check on a couple big clients. The furniture business never sleeps."

"Unless you're selling beds," Howie offered.

Sid glanced at Howie with what Angela thought was a look of annoyance. Then suddenly, he burst out laughing. "That's a good one, kid. By the way, nice flannel." He turned back to Big Lou. "But of course, I can't be in Chicago without getting some of your deep dish."

"And will you see Karla Kopeki while you're here?"

"Are you kidding? Mom would roast me alive if I failed to visit her best friend in the world. In fact, I'm going over there right now to share some of this delicious pie with her."

"Well, give Karla my best. And Sid, don't be a stranger. You may be a Bills fan, but your money spends just the same."

Sid's phone buzzed, and he stepped away to answer it. Big Lou turned back to the booth. "Well, kids. Enjoy your pizza, and best of luck with the whole nickname thing. And if the winner's not Big Lou's Pizza, I'm sure you'll come up with something that's just as good." He walked back toward Sid, who was still on the phone. Angela noticed Sid was agitated by something.

"I think I've got it," Howie said.

Angela turned back to her friend. "Got what?"

"The perfectly ridiculous school nickname. A name that's so bad, it just might be good."

Howie waited while Jamie, Norah, and Angela all looked at him, then finally when the anticipation was just right, he motioned with his hands as if he was unveiling a big surprise. "I give you Beveridge Middle School, home of the... Green Flannel."

As soon as the words came out of his mouth, Angela knew it was the perfect name. Beyond ridiculous. Not offensive at all. And utterly unique.

"So, we go from being the Beveridge Eagles to the

Beveridge Green Flannel?" Jamie asked. "I think it's sort of genius. What do you think, Angela?"

"It's perfect. Norah?"

"What can I say? My best friend's not completely useless. I like it too."

Angela turned back toward Sid Granger, who was now hustling out of the pizza shop while Big Lou walked their way with a concerned look on his face.

"Something wrong, Big Lou?"

He nodded. "Sid just got a call from Karla Kopeki. Someone broke into her apartment today."

"That's terrible."

"It's worse than terrible. Something was stolen. Something very dear to her. The whole thing makes me just sick." Big Lou walked away sadly.

"That's awful," Jamie said. "Mrs. Kopeki is really nice."

"Mrs. Kopeki?" Angela said, trying to retrieve a memory. "Isn't that the woman who bakes chocolate chip cookies on Wednesdays and leaves her window open for all of us to smell them?"

"That's her all right," Howie said. "And not only are her cookies great, but Big Lou and Jamie are right. She's super nice. I'm so sorry this happened to her."

"Well," Angela said, "maybe we don't have to just feel

bad for her. Maybe we can do something about it."

"Like what?" Norah asked.

"Like, we're the Science Inspectors. We already helped Mr. Bannister out a few weeks ago. Maybe we could help Mrs. Kopecki too."

Norah frowned. "Didn't you just convince us to join you in your grand scheme to get one over on Nina Marcus? A plan you still haven't fully explained, and one that we have to do this week? And now you want to add an investigation on top of that?"

Angela shrugged. "What can I say? I'm special that way. Come on. Let's just stop over at Mrs. Kopecki's and take a look. Maybe we can figure something out. Unless, Norah, you think you're not smart enough to solve another case?"

Norah narrowed her eyes at Angela. "Your feeble attempt at reverse psychology will not work on me, Moretti."

Angela stood up and left money on the table for her share of the pizza. "I think it just did. Come on, guys. We've got a new case to solve."

CHAPTER 3

NOT ON MY WATCH

By the time they entered Mrs. Kopecki's building ten minutes later, a small crowd had formed on the second floor. The man they had seen at Big Lou's, Sid Granger, was there next to a lovely pear-shaped woman who was clearly shaken up. A small mousy woman with thick red eyeglasses stood next to her. A young couple with a baby stood behind them. They all stared at a door with the number 23 on it, which was slightly ajar. Angela heard movement inside. The small woman with the red glasses turned to them.

"Captain Healy's going through her apartment as we speak." She patted the pear-shaped woman on the shoulder. "Thankfully, Karla called him right away. The two of them go way back. We all do, really." She leaned over to Karla. "And who'd you call after that?"

"I called you, of course."

"That's right. You called me, which makes sense. It's

not like I'm in charge around here, but I keep my eye on things, that's for certain. Edna Henson reporting for duty, sir. And Karla says to me, 'Oh, Edna, someone stole Bobby's watch. They broke in and stole his watch.'"

Edna looked at the family, at Sid, and at Angela and her friends and waited. Finally, Angela took the bait.

"Who's Bobby?"

Edna patted Karla on the back again. "Who's Bobby? Only the single greatest husband who ever lived and the love of Karla's life. Bobby Kopecki's been gone... oh, what has it been, Karla? A dozen years now?"

"Fifteen," Karla said in a whisper as she continued to stare at the door.

"Fifteen years?" Edna said with surprise. Then she shook her head somberly and made the sign of the cross. "Where does the time go? So, after you called me, who'd you call then, Karla?"

Karla finally stopped staring at her apartment and turned toward the small crowd. "I called Sid because I knew he was coming over. I had gone to bridge club like I always do on Tuesdays. Sid was coming over with some pizza for dinner, and I was anxious to spend a few minutes putting myself together before he arrived. But when I got to my door, I noticed it was open, which was odd. I never leave my door open. I always double-check.

I'm quite fastidious that way."

"Of that I can attest." Edna nodded. "Like I said, I keep an eye on things around here. And one thing I'll tell you is that Karla Kopecki always locks her door."

"My heart started beating fast. Like, really thumping out of my chest. I knew someone had been in my apartment. Maybe they were *still* in my apartment. I thought about going up to Edna's apartment first."

"Which I would have understood. Like I said, Edna Henson, reporting for duty."

"But I didn't."

Edna shook her head. "No, she didn't."

"I grabbed a little bottle of pepper spray I keep in my purse. Bobby bought me some a long time ago. I never used it on a person. I did use it on a dog one time. A vicious little poodle that came at me. Grabbed my grocery bag and tore it from my hands. That pepper spray worked just like Bobby said it would, so I always keep some with me. I grabbed it and went into my apartment, but... nobody was there."

"That's when Karla noticed something," Edna said.

"That's right. I looked over at the buffet cabinet in my dining room like I always do when I enter my apartment, but it was gone. The watch was gone. The watch I'd given to Bobby so many years ago."

"And that's when you called Captain Healy, right?" Edna prodded.

"That's right. I called Captain Healy, who said he'd be over right away. Then I called Edna. Then I called Sid, and finally, I called Sid's mom, Alma."

Sid nodded. "My mom and Karla go way back too."

Karla nodded. "Alma and I became best friends on the first day of first grade."

"And remain so to this day," Sid said.

"Even though Alma moved to Buffalo twenty years ago. Whenever Sid's in town, he brings me some Big Lou's. Sid's good to me that way."

The door to Apartment 23 swung open, and Captain Healy walked out. He looked around at the small crowd, and when his eyes settled on Angela and her friends, he got a slightly perturbed look on his face. Then he turned his focus to Mrs. Kopecki.

"I looked at the lock. No sign of forced entry. Meaning, whoever did this either had a key or is very good at picking locks. Are you sure the watch is the only thing that was stolen?"

"No, I'm not sure. I do keep a hundred dollars in an envelope under my mattress. That's my emergency fund. But I didn't check that."

"Be sure you do, then let me know. Your television's still

there. So is your iPad. I noticed a couple pieces of crystal that are probably worth something, but those were left alone as well. My guess? One of these street thieves broke in, saw the watch, thought it looked valuable, then got spooked and left in a hurry. That's probably why he left the door open. I'll be honest with you, Karla—these types of cases are very difficult to solve. I'll file a report, then I'll have some of my people check with the local pawn shops to see if anyone comes in looking to unload a watch."

Karla shook her head. "I can't believe a pawn shop would be interested in a broken watch."

Captain Healy frowned. "Excuse me. Are you saying the watch is broken?"

"It hasn't worked since the day I bought it for Bobby."

Captain Healy closed his eyes and massaged the temples of his head with his fingers and thumbs.

"You called me because someone stole a watch that's never worked, not ever?"

"That doesn't give someone a right to steal it."

Captain Healy let out an exasperated sigh. "I'll file the report and we'll check into local pawn shops. But if, as you say, the watch is broken, I'm afraid there's just not much we can do."

Then Captain Healy left, but not before he shot Angela a look of clear annoyance.

The young family went back into their apartment while Edna Henson folded her arms disapprovingly. "You'd think Captain Healy would be more helpful than that."

Karla sighed. "He does have a point. I can't really expect the criminal justice system to care that much about a watch that doesn't even work."

"Well, Karla," Sid said, "would you like me to come in and stay with you for a bit?"

"That's kind of you, Sid. But no. I just don't feel like it now."

He tried to hand the pizza box to her, but she shook her head.

"And I'm sorry to say I don't much have an appetite anymore. I think... I think I just want to be by myself. Thank you for coming over, and give your dear mother a hug from me."

"I will. For sure. And I'll be in town until the end of the week checking in with clients, so if you need something from me, don't hesitate to call."

Sid left while Edna and Karla spoke a little while longer. Angela and her friends circled up.

"I think that's our cue to leave as well," Jamie said.

"Agreed," Norah said. "Moretti needs to explain the rest of this reverse psychology plan to us."

"We can't leave," Angela said.

"Why can't we?" Norah asked.

"Because you heard Captain Healy. He barely did anything in there. And once he found out the watch didn't even work? Well, you saw his face. He's not about to lift a finger to help her."

"Then, and I hate to sound uncharitable here," Norah said, "why should we care so much about it? The watch is broken. Meaning, it's worthless."

"That's not exactly true," Howie said.

Norah gave Howie a look similar to the one Captain Healy had given Angela.

"Sorry to disagree with you, best friend, but the watch is clearly very valuable to Mrs. Kopecki because it reminds her of her husband."

Angela nodded. "And if the police aren't going to do anything about it, the Science Inspectors should do what we can to help. What do we have to lose?"

Norah and Jamie looked at each other, and Jamie's face was the first to relax. Finally, Norah said, "Okay. But I just want to go on the record as saying that I think this is a waste of our resources."

"So noted," Angela said. "And if you end up being right—"

"Which I usually am."

"Then you will have the satisfaction of saying I told you so."

Edna Henson walked up the stairs to her apartment, and Karla Kopecki went back into hers. But before she could close the door, Angela said, "Pardon me, Mrs. Kopecki."

Mrs. Kopecki turned around. "Yes, dear? What is it?"

"You don't know me, but I'm Angela Moretti, Tony Moretti's daughter and Nonna's granddaughter."

Mrs. Kopecki looked at Angela, then placed a gentle hand against her cheek and patted it. "Of course you are. Has anyone ever told you how much you look like...?" Her voice trailed off.

"My mother?" Angela said. "Yes, I get that a lot. Anyway, I'm so sorry for what you're going through, and I'll just cut to the chase. I got the distinct impression that Captain Healy isn't going to put much effort into helping you."

"I got that impression as well."

"That's where we come in." Angela turned and gestured to her friends. "We're the Science Inspectors, and we like to use our science and detective skills to help solve problems just like this, the ones the police don't care much about."

"What are you saying exactly?"

"If you'll go through your story one more time and let us take a look at your apartment, we'll do whatever we can to help solve your case."

"My case?"

"Yes, Mrs. Kopecki. The case of the broken watch."

CHAPTER 4

A BAFFLING BUFFET

Norah, Howie, and Jamie squeezed onto Mrs. Kopeki's floral-printed love seat. Angela sat on an old wooden rocking chair, and Mrs. Kopeki settled into a burgundy La-Z-Boy recliner.

"Well, it's like I said. I'd just come back from bridge club."

"And this is something you do on Tuesdays?" Angela asked.

She nodded. "From 2:30 to 5:30. Every week."

"And do you ever miss?" Angela asked.

"Not unless I'm sick, and I haven't been sick in... oh, I don't know. Ten years. I'm kind of like the postal service. Neither snow nor rain nor heat or gloom of night stays this old woman from the swift completion of her bridge playing."

Jamie's eyes widened as if he understood where Angela was going with this. "Meaning, anybody who knows you knows that you're out of your apartment every Tuesday."

"I suppose that's true. We play bridge down at the VFW."

Howie's forehead scrunched. "What's the VFW?"

"It stands for Veterans of Foreign Wars," Jamie explained. "My grandfather fought in the Vietnam War, and he's a member."

Mrs. Kopeki nodded. "That's right, dear. My Bobby was in Vietnam as well. A group of us wives have played cards there forever. It was actually poker back in the day, but eventually we learned bridge, which is quite a bit more interesting than poker, if you ask me." She grabbed a small quilt that was folded over the armrest and laid it on her lap. "It's quite a stretch of the legs from the VFW back to my building, and I don't usually come home until close to six. Well, as soon as I came up the stairs to the second floor, I could see my door was open just a bit. And like Edna said before, that never happens. I always lock my door. Always."

Angela said, "That's when you grabbed your can of pepper spray and walked into the apartment?"

"That's right. I expected to find someone in here. I was scared, I tell you. As scared as I've been in a long while."

"But then you quickly noticed that your watch was gone," Norah said. "Why, if you were so scared, did you notice the missing watch?"

Mrs. Kopeki shrugged. "That's where I always look when I enter the apartment."

She turned and pointed to her dining room. There was a small round wooden table. Beyond it, hugging the wall, was a maple buffet cabinet. There was some kind of pedestal in the center, and on that pedestal was nothing.

"I keep Bobby's watch right there on top of the buffet cabinet his parents gave to us as a wedding present. It's the first thing I see when I come into the apartment. It keeps me company when I sit at the table with my morning coffee and newspaper. It's there in the evenings when I have my supper. I suppose having the watch close by is like having Bobby near me."

"Forgive me for asking this, Mrs. Kopeki, but why exactly is the watch so meaningful?" Howie asked. "You did tell Captain Healy that it's broken, right?"

Mrs. Kopeki smiled. "That's part of what makes it so special. Bobby and I met at a dance before he went to Vietnam. I'll never forget that night. This handsome young man walked over to me, and do you know what he said?"

Angela leaned forward. "What?"

"He said, 'Miss, would you allow me to dance with the prettiest girl in the room?'"

"That's a good line," Jamie said.

Mrs. Kopeki nodded. "That's what I thought. So, I agreed, and Bobby and I danced the whole night long and we kissed in the moonlight. I fell in love with him on the spot. We spent every possible minute with each other until he left for Vietnam, and when he got back, we got married. Not long after that, I was pregnant with our first child. Bobby needed a job to support our family, so he took the only job he could find, working in a local meat-packing plant. It was hard work and didn't pay so well, and Bobby was always looking for another opportunity.

"He finally got himself an interview at a big insurance company downtown. Problem was, we didn't really have enough money for the type of fancy clothes one needs for a job like that, so Bobby found himself an old suit at the local thrift shop that fit well enough, but between you and me, it was a bit shabby."

Mrs. Kopecki leaned back in her recliner and sighed as if suddenly lost in a different time many years before. "I wanted something to spruce him up, so to speak, and I found it at a garage sale. An absolutely stunning wristwatch that the owner was practically giving away. You should have seen Bobby's face when I gave it to him. He was on cloud nine. And the next morning, he walked out of our apartment with so much confidence and energy, I just knew he would get that job."

Mrs. Kopecki stopped and looked at Angela and her friends as if she was waiting for them to catch up. "But there was just one problem."

Howie raised his hand excitedly. "You told Captain Healy that the watch never worked."

Mrs. Kopecki smiled. "You were paying attention. Of course, neither Bobby nor I knew that, so when Bobby walked into that big insurance company for his interview, he was told to walk right back out the door because he was late. Well, Bobby was furiously disappointed, as you can imagine. There he was on the sidewalk in downtown Chicago apparently expressing this disappointment when a man in a three-piece suit stopped and asked him what was wrong."

"And?" Angela asked.

"Bobby told him. And not just about the broken watch and the missed opportunity, but about the challenges of coming back from the war and getting a job that was good enough to support a family. And then the craziest thing happened. That man just happened to run an investment firm, was a Korean War vet, and hired Bobby right there on the spot. Bobby worked for that company the rest of his life. It was the best thing that ever happened, and it only happened because of that broken watch."

"Wow," is all Angela could say.

"Wow is right. You see, I know that old watch isn't valuable in the traditional sense, but it's incredibly valuable to me because it reminds me of my husband. And I can't for the life of me imagine who would have stolen it."

"I can't either," Howie said.

Norah tapped her pen against her notebook. "You said it looked like a fancy watch."

"You bet it did. That's why I bought it in the first place."

"And you didn't know it was broken when you bought it."

"Correct," Mrs. Kopecki said.

"So, chances are, the thief didn't know either. He just saw a fancy-looking watch and took it," Norah said.

"And you're sure nothing else was taken?" Angela pressed.

Mrs. Kopecki scanned the room, then got up from her chair and walked to her bedroom. Ten seconds later, she was back.

"The hundred dollars under my mattress is still there, and I can't see anything else missing."

"Then do you mind if we take a look and examine the crime scene?" Angela asked. "We have some experience with this sort of thing, and we might be able to find something that can help us figure it out."

"I can't tell you how much I appreciate this," the old woman said. "I wish there was something I could do for you in return."

"I think there is," Angela said. "On Wednesdays, there's an especially delicious smell that comes from your apartment."

"Do you like chocolate chip cookies?"

"I sure do, so we'll make you a deal. We'll do everything we can to find your watch, and in exchange, we would love to try your cookies."

The old woman smiled. "It's a deal. Now I'll stay out of your way while you kids look around."

Mrs. Kopecki turned on the television and sat back in her chair while Angela pulled her crime investigation supplies from her blue backpack. She handed gloves to everyone, then gave them plastic evidence bags along with magnifying glasses and tweezers.

"Remember, we're looking for anything the thief may have left behind that might lead to his or her identity.

Take a picture of it. Then bag it and tag it."

While Norah, Howie, and Jamie looked for physical evidence, Angela dusted for prints on and around the buffet cabinet. When she finished, she dusted for prints on both sides of the apartment's front door. Then she asked Mrs. Kopeki if she could take her fingerprints. The old woman agreed.

"You really are quite official. Where did you learn to do all this?"

"Books first. Then I watched a bunch of YouTube videos. By the way, have you had many visitors to your apartment lately?"

Mrs. Kopecki thought about it, then shook her head. "Not for a while. In fact, Sid was going to be my first guest in the last month."

"Perfect. Then the only fingerprints I find in this apartment should belong to you. And if I find someone else's, they probably belong to our thief."

CHAPTER 5

PASSING THE TEST TUBE

They were back at Howie's lab examining their evidence when a particular bag stood out.

"Who found this one?" Angela asked. The bag contained tiny bits of a white crystal-like substance.

"I did," Jamie said. "On the carpet right in front of the buffet cabinet." He grabbed his phone and pulled up the relevant pictures. The substance could be seen in three different photos.

"Any idea what it is?" Angela asked.

Howie snatched the bag out of her hand, opened it, and slid a finger inside until he grabbed one of the specks. Then he pulled it out and said "I have a pretty good idea" right before he opened his mouth. Norah slapped him on the back of his head.

"Don't you dare eat that, you ninny."

"Hey, that hurt. Besides, I bet you a hundred dollars

this is salt, which is totally harmless."

"Sure, it might be salt. Probably is. But what if it's not?" Norah asked. "What if this is the time you're wrong, and it's actually poisonous?"

"I didn't really think about that."

"You sure didn't. But I have an idea. What if we had access to a scientific lab where we could run tests to see what the substance actually is? Oh, wait. We do. And we're standing in it."

"How do we test to see if it's salt?" Angela asked.

"Salt dissolves in water, doesn't it?" Jamie asked.

"Correct," Norah confirmed. "Creating a solution of salt water."

"And further," Howie continued, "if you were to take that salt water and boil the water, the water would evaporate, and the only thing left would be the salt."

Howie filled a test tube with water, then emptied the bag of crystals into the test tube and stirred it up just a little until the substance disappeared into the water.

"So far, so good," Norah said.

Then Jamie lit a Bunsen burner, and Angela placed the test tube with the solution over the burner. A minute later, the water started boiling, and another five minutes later, all the water had evaporated into steam. But something was left behind.

A white powdery substance.

Howie smiled. "Like I said, salt."

"Then let's consider the scientific method," Norah said. "As a first step, we have observed salt at the crime scene. And that leads to step two, thinking of interesting questions."

Jamie grabbed the beaker out of Howie's hand and studied it. "Namely, what was salt doing on the carpet of our crime scene?"

"And coming up with an answer to that question could lead to our first hypothesis about who committed this crime," Angela said.

"I think I've got it," Howie said. "Salt was on the carpet because a salt monster stole the watch."

"What exactly is a salt monster?" Jamie asked.

"Duh. It's a monster made entirely of salt. And if such a monster existed, it would definitely leave salt behind. Plus, Captain Healy said there was no sign of forced entry. Well, I can assure you that a salt monster could easily slip into an apartment without damaging the door."

"Are you finished?" Norah asked. "Because in the actual world where there's no such thing as salt monsters, I'd prefer we give real answers to these questions." She glanced at the wall clock. "I'd also prefer to get home, finish my homework, and study for my history test."

She looked at Angela. "So, misfit, you've got us on another case, trying to come up with interesting questions about salt all the while we execute some grand plan to make Beveridge into the home of the Green Flannel. You think maybe we've bitten off a little more than we can chew?"

Angela thought it over. Norah might be right. In fact, she was usually right, but Angela was usually stubborn. And though that stubbornness could get her in trouble, it was also sometimes her great superpower because she hated to give up.

"No, I actually don't," Angela finally replied. "Because I know we're up for the challenge. No matter what happens, we can figure it out. And we can do it because..." She laughed maniacally and pointed to Howie, who immediately understood the cue.

He bellowed, "There's a scientific method to our madness!"

# # #

Later that night, Angela sent out an email outlining the multi-tiered approach to what the Science Inspectors were calling "Operation Green Flannel." And the next morning as students milled about the quad, Angela made her way to the center of the quad near the flagpole where Nina Marcus and her friends assembled each day before and after school.

“Hey, Nina,” she said, interrupting the trio of girls as they were staring at their phones and giggling. Nina looked up and when she saw who it was, an ugly sneer appeared on her face.

“What do *you* want?” she said, emphasizing “you” like it was some kind of curse word.

“Oh, I just wanted to say great job. I never did like ‘Eagles,’ and I’m happy we’re finally going to have a cool name like ‘Rubies.’ Thanks!”

The key to their operation was to use reverse psychology to manipulate Nina into throwing her support behind Green Flannel. It wasn’t going to be easy, but Angela thought a good first step was to show Nina how much she liked Nina’s idea. It was no secret that Nina didn’t like Angela very much. If Angela liked Rubies, that might be enough on its own to change Nina’s mind.

Nina appeared to be offended Angela would dare to speak with her. “Fine. Whatever,” was all she said in reply.

It appeared Nina would need more persuading. This

was where Angela needed to be careful. *Don't press too hard. Just enough.*

"I'm also glad that the administration likes the new name."

Nina's eyes snapped up from her phone. "What do you mean?"

"I heard Dean Dunwoody and the principal talking about it yesterday. They love the name. They were worried the students were going to choose something edgy or dangerous. They're both really glad we went in such a safe direction. Dean Dunwoody even said rubies are his wife's birthstone. Anyway, good job. See you later!"

The sneer was gone from Nina's face, and it was replaced by a different sort of expression. Angela couldn't quite nail it down but if she had to guess, she'd say it was something very close to uncertainty. Step one of Operation Green Flannel was complete.

Once they convinced Nina to stop advocating for the Rubies, they would need to convince her to throw her support behind the Green Flannel. That would be significantly more challenging. Thankfully, the Science Inspectors were humongous nerds with significant resources of the brain.

It just so happened that over the past year, Howie had

been recording Dean Dunwoody's voice and then plugging it into a program where Dean Dunwoody's real voice could read any script that Howie had. That morning, Howie and Norah were in charge of recording Dean Dunwoody saying "green flannel," which they did by challenging him to answer a riddle. Dean Dunwoody was a sucker for riddles. Turns out he didn't even understand this one. Fact was, neither did they. He grumpily dismissed them, but not before they had exactly what they needed.

By lunchtime, Howie had created his masterpiece—Dean Dunwoody's voice saying, "'Green Flannel' is the last nickname I would ever want for this school."

"Nice work, Howie," Jamie said. "That sounds just like him."

"Because it is him," Howie said. "I keep trying to tell you that."

"I just meant, it sounds great. Well done."

"I agree," Angela said. "The challenge is getting this into Nina's hands. And that's where you come in, Jamie, because you're just a little cooler than we are."

Jamie smirked. "I'm a lot cooler than you are, but I don't think I should be penalized for it. I don't like Nina any more than you do."

"Fair enough," Angela said. "But you've got a better

shot at pulling this off than we do. Want to go over it again?"

He stood up from the table. "No way. I've got this. Howie, just send me the file."

The truth, an uncomfortable truth Angela didn't love to admit, was that Nina liked Jamie. The way she looked at him. Giggled around him. Twirled her hair when she saw him. It was obvious, and that annoyed Angela to no end. Nina was the worst. Times ten. Jamie was a good and decent kid. Her friend. She didn't want those worlds to collide, but if it was in the service of the greater good? And if that greater good was getting one over on Nina? Well, in that case, Angela could tolerate it. Barely.

Jamie strutted as cool as he could over to Nina's table. Then he bent over and said something, and even from twenty feet away, Angela could hear Nina giggle and saw her tuck a strand of hair behind her ear.

Classic signs.

Which made Angela want to barf.

She watched as Jamie and Nina talked for a few more minutes before Jamie took out his phone and held it toward Nina. She listened to whatever was on the phone, then Jamie talked some more. A little while later, Jamie walked back to their table.

"So?" Norah said. "Do you need to run through a

decontamination unit of some sort? I think that's the longest conversation a normal human being has ever had with Nina."

"I don't like Nina any more than you do."

Angela felt her cheeks getting warm. "You sure about that?"

Jamie looked at her firmly. "Yes, I'm sure about that. I set the trap and I think I did it convincingly. I mentioned that I love the name 'Rubies,' but then I told her how weird Dunwoody was being about everything. A guy from the football team taped the dean going off about how much he hated the idea of us being called the 'Green Flannel.' I figured Nina would know something about it since she was the most powerful girl in school. She said she hadn't heard about it. And that was it."

"So, what's next for Operation Green Flannel?" Howie asked.

"Nothing for today," Angela said. "We press our advantage tomorrow. But I do have a nice surprise for you all. I received a text from Mrs. Kopecki—who, by the way, has mad emoji game for an old timer. She said that it's baking day and wanted to know if we might be interested in coming by after school."

"And what did you tell her?" Howie said excitedly.

"That there's an interesting hypothesis out there that

she makes the very best chocolate chip cookies in all of Brundon Park. Since we're the Science Inspectors, I say it's our job to go test that out."

CHAPTER 6

RECIPE FOR CONFUSION

Angela was already enjoying her second delicious cookie when Howie exclaimed, “Hypothesis confirmed. These are definitely the best chocolate chip cookies in all of Brundon Park.”

Jamie nodded eagerly while Norah held up a finger. “This is an excellent cookie for sure. But this being science and all, in order to proclaim these the very best cookies, we would have to rule out any other hypothesis.”

Mrs. Kopecki smirked. “In other words, how can you know for sure if you haven’t tried all the other great chocolate chip cookies in the neighborhood?”

Norah smiled. “Exactly.” Then she took another bite of her cookie.

Mrs. Kopecki stood up, walked to her kitchen, and came back with a purple ribbon, handing it to Norah. “Is this sufficient evidence?”

Norah examined it and then read aloud, "First place, Cookie Baking. Brundon Park Festival." She looked up at Mrs. Kopecki. "You won this last year?"

"And the four years before that as well," she said proudly.

"Well then, as long as everyone else agrees, I do too," Norah said. "Best cookie in Brundon Park."

Mrs. Kopecki sat back down in her comfortable chair. "I wouldn't say *everyone* agrees. Especially not Sofia."

"Who's Sofia?" Angela asked.

"Sofia Pantano. She lives on the fourth floor of this building. She's come in either second or third place behind me the last four years, and she's been none too happy about it. But that doesn't bother me too much. Sofia and I've known each other a long time, and she's never cared for me."

"How can that be?" Howie asked. "You're just a sweet old lady."

Mrs. Kopecki glared at him. "Old?"

Howie's face started turning red. "Oops. Did I say that out loud?"

"You did."

"That was rude of me."

"Yes, it was," Mrs. Kopecki said, her face softening. "But also true. I am old, even though I don't try to be.

And I'm not always very sweet, even though I definitely try to be. Sofia and I—we're a little like oil and water. And I'll give you one hint—I ain't the oil."

"Are you saying she's a little extra?" Angela asked.

Mrs. Kopecki leaned forward. "Extra? I'm not sure I follow."

"It's how young people say that some folks are just too much in one way or another."

She leaned back and thought. "Hmmm. Sofia Pantano. She always dresses to the nines. Perfume for days. Fake fur coats in the winters, and the longest nails you ever did see. And boy oh boy, does that woman have opinions. Yes, I'd say she's quite a bit extra, but that's not the entire reason for our feud. It's got more to do with her husband, Glen."

"What about him?" Howie asked.

Mrs. Kopecki waved her hand in front of her face. "I ought not to gossip. Angela, you said you kids wanted to follow up with me on a few things?"

Angela nodded, then swallowed her last bite of cookie. "We heard your version of things last night and examined your apartment. We took fingerprints and collected samples of fibers, hairs, things like that. But something Jamie found was particularly noteworthy."

Jamie showed Mrs. Kopecki his phone, and the woman looked at the photo on it through the bottom part of her bifocals. Then Jamie pointed.

"We found salt on the carpet in front of the buffet cabinet."

She squinted as if to verify for herself. Then she looked up at Jamie. "And?"

"And we thought that was interesting," Norah said.

"And that led us to our question," Angela continued. "Can you think of why salt would be on the floor right where your husband's watch was stolen?"

Mrs. Kopecki thought about it and then shook her head. "I can't."

"Okay," Norah said. "You use salt whenever you cook or bake?"

"Naturally."

"And did you cook or bake yesterday?"

"Not really. I had a couple of Eggo waffles for breakfast, then picked up a pastrami on rye down at the VFW while I played bridge. I was going to finish off the night with a slice of Big Lou's, but I lost my appetite after the robbery. I didn't bake until this morning when I made these cookies."

"Is it possible you cooked or baked with salt the day before yesterday?" Jamie asked.

"I definitely did."

"And is there any way that you might have dropped

some salt on the floor in front of the buffet cabinet?"

"No."

"It's not possible?" Norah asked.

"Not possible," Mrs. Kopecki confirmed. "Remember how Edna said I was fastidious about locking my door? I'm not that way about everything in my life, but I am about some things. Cooking and baking, for instance. I double- and triple-check my recipes. Even the recipes I've used my whole life. I measure precisely. It would drive you crazy to watch me measure out my sugar. I do not spill. And I keep my kitchen immaculate."

Howie seemed disappointed by the answer, but Angela was not. In fact, it excited her because this unexplained salt was precisely the kind of thing that might be a clue about the thief.

Observations lead to interesting questions that lead to hypotheses.

"Mrs. Kopecki, can you help us think about how the salt might have gotten there?"

The old woman's eyes opened wide, and she stood up from her chair. "I keep my kitchen immaculate!"

"We know," Norah said. "You just got done telling us."

"No—this morning, I noticed there was a little bit of salt on my counter. I thought it was odd because, as I told you,

I don't leave messes. But I ignored it, wiped it up, then reached into my salt container, where I also keep my..." Her breath caught in her throat, and she hustled to her kitchen in a bit of a panic. Angela and the others followed her. Mrs. Kopecki was right—her kitchen was immaculate.

At the moment, Mrs. Kopecki was looking inside a yellow ceramic container. There were five similar containers on her counter, all slightly different sizes. The kind people often use to store sugar, flour, brown sugar, and yes, salt.

She pulled a small index card out of the container and held it up in the air. "My secret chocolate chip cookie recipe! I keep it hidden."

Angela looked at the others, who exchanged similarly bewildered looks.

Mrs. Kopecki must have noticed their confusion. She turned back around and grabbed a small recipe box, the kind full of index cards. Then she explained. "I'm paranoid, okay? So, sue me. This is a special chocolate chip cookie recipe that my mother gave me. And yes, there is a secret ingredient, and no, I'm not going to share it with you. I promised my mom I would take the secret to my grave, so I never keep the recipe with the others. I stick it in my salt container, where I figure no one would ever look."

Angela stepped toward Mrs. Kopecki, who quickly stuck the recipe behind her back. "Don't worry, Mrs. Kopecki. I don't want to look at your recipe." Then she turned to the counter and looked at the containers. "Guys, I have a hypothesis. What if our thief wasn't here to steal the watch?"

Norah, Jamie, and Howie squeezed in the small kitchen alongside her.

"What if the thief was here to steal the recipe?" Jamie said.

"Exactly."

Mrs. Kopecki frowned. "But the recipe's still here."

"Of course it is," Norah said. "Because your thief didn't need to take that card. He or she just needed to take a picture of it."

Mrs. Kopecki put a hand to her mouth as she gasped.

"Someone came into your apartment when they knew you'd be gone," Howie began.

"For the main purpose of stealing your prize-winning recipe," Angela said.

"And just as they found the recipe hidden in the salt container..." Norah continued.

"That's when they noticed this fancy-looking watch in the dining room," Jamie said.

"There must have been some salt on the recipe card,"

Angela continued. "They had the card in their hand as they walked the few feet from the kitchen to the dining room, where they spilled salt on the floor as they grabbed the watch."

"Then they took pictures of the recipe and put the card back in the salt container," Howie concluded.

Mrs. Kopecki and the Science Inspectors all stood there thinking it over. Mrs. Kopecki was the first one to say something. "It makes sense."

Angela nodded. "It actually does. But if we're right, that's got to narrow down the list of suspects. In fact, based on what you just told us, our list might be down to one."

"Sofia Pantano," Jamie said.

Mrs. Kopecki's eyes darted back and forth as she took in this information.

"Any idea if Mrs. Pantano is home this time of day?" Angela asked.

"We're not exactly friends, but this is a small neighborhood and we do live in the same building. You get accustomed to people's habits. Most days, she and her husband go down to Happy Holland Country Club. Her husband plays golf while she plays tennis. I swear the only reason she does it is so she can wear those outfits. Do you really think Sofia might have done this?"

"I don't know, but I think it's a pretty good hypothesis," Angela said. "Now we just need to prove it. Thanks, Mrs. Kopecki, for the cookies. We'll be in touch."

The Science Inspectors left the old woman's apartment, but instead of heading downstairs, Angela took the stairs up two by two.

Norah called from behind, "Wait, Angela, wait. Don't do anything stupid."

But Angela ignored her, which was the kind of thing she usually did when she was determined. As her friends hurried to catch up with her on the fourth floor, Angela knocked on Apartment 47.

"You really think this is a good idea?" Jamie asked.

"Probably not, but for the moment, it's the only one I've got."

"She's not just going to admit she's a thief," Howie said.

"Probably not," Angela agreed. "But based on her reaction, at least we'll know if she's lying. And then we'll know if we're on the right path." She turned and knocked again, but nobody came.

"Mrs. Kopecki's probably right," Norah observed. "They must be down at the country club. Come on—time to figure out the next step for Operation Green Flannel."

"You bet," Angela said while taking off her blue

backpack. “But not before I collect a little more evidence.” She took out her kit, then quickly brushed the doorknob and the front door for fingerprints. She found three sets, lifted them off with her special tape, and then bagged each one and identified them. Then she looked at her friends and smiled. “Maybe Sofia Pantano’s more than a little extra. Maybe she’s also a thief. Who wants to go to the lab and find out?”

CHAPTER 7

CONFECTION INSPECTION

Angela found the fingerprint she'd lifted off the cabinet, the print that did not belong to Mrs. Kopecki. She found the three different fingerprints she'd lifted off the Pantanos' apartment door, along with Mrs. Kopecki's fingerprint. Then Howie scanned all five with his high-resolution scanner and loaded them up to the lab's fingerprint program. Five minutes later, they had their answer.

"Sorry, Angela," Howie said. "No match."

"Huh," she replied as she stared at the results on the large computer screen against the wall. "I was hoping for an easy win. The stolen recipe hypothesis made so much sense."

"It still does make sense," Jamie said.

"Correct," Norah agreed. "Remember, you didn't disprove that hypothesis at all. You didn't even eliminate Sofia Pantano as a suspect. All we proved is the fingerprint on that cabinet does not belong to Mrs. Kopecki or any of the three fingerprints you found on the Pantanos' door."

"You're right."

"You really don't have to remind me, Moretti. I'm almost always right."

"Super humble as well," Jamie remarked. "I still like the stolen recipe hypothesis, especially with the contest coming up in two weeks. But maybe we need to broaden our pool of suspects beyond Sofia Pantano. The contest is sponsored by Gloria Goddard. She might know of some other women capable of recipe theft."

"Oooh," Howie said. "Candy!"

Norah looked up from her notebook. "We just ate cookies, and now you want candy?"

"First of all, I always want candy. Second, this is about conducting a serious investigation, but if in the course of this investigation, one of those gargantuan gumdrops should fall into my mouth? That's just a delightful perk of the job."

# # #

Howie and Jamie were deciding between gargantuan gumdrops and stupendous suckers when Gloria

Goddard appeared from the back of the store. She looked right at Angela and smiled.

"I was busy making caramels when I saw you coming in on my security feed, and I just had to say hello."

Gloria Goddard looked exactly like someone should look when they owned a place as ridiculous as Gloria's Gargantuan Gumdrops. Her hair was big and bold and almost certainly required a dangerous level of hairspray. Her makeup was loud and colorful. And if possible, her personality was even bigger than her look. The woman was passionate, a little bit like Angela's own mother had been—a little bit like Angela was—and she oscillated between happy and sad like a human yo-yo. On this particular day, she seemed content.

"Well, hello back," Angela said.

Gloria motioned for Angela to come closer and then leaned over the counter. "I've been meaning to chat with you."

Uh-oh, Angela thought. This couldn't be good. Except... Gloria didn't seem angry. Not one bit.

"You probably heard that Mr. Bannister and I have been dating again the last few weeks."

Angela held back a smile. "I did hear about that. How are things going?"

Her cheeks flushed a bit. She batted her considerable eyelashes and sighed the way Angela had seen actresses sometimes do in the old movies she watched with Nonna.

"It's going amazingly well. And that's actually why I wanted to speak with you. You see, I happened to have a conversation with his son, Chris, the other day."

"Oh?" Angela said, remembering their previous case.

Gloria placed her hand gently on Angela's arm.

"And dear, I just wanted to say thank you. Chris mentioned that you encouraged him to give that old coot a kick in the rear. That you somehow knew that I still loved him, and that he was about to let something really great pass him by if he didn't make amends."

"He said all that?"

She nodded, and Angela noticed a tear in the corner of her eye.

"Men can be awfully dumb sometimes," Gloria said. "But they're pretty special as well. And me and old Mr. Bannister? Well, I owe you one."

"I don't know what to say."

"Well, I do. And it's something I never, ever say." She walked over to the cash register, grabbed what looked like a large drumstick, then turned around and smashed it against a gong that Angela had somehow never noticed before. The noise and vibration shook the entire store so much that Angela could feel her teeth chatter back and forth.

"Attention, Science Inspectors. That is what you call yourselves, correct?"

Norah made a face. "I'm still hoping that 'Norah and the Misfits' catches on, but for now we answer to both."

Gloria stood ramrod straight and cocked her head back like she was suddenly one of those guards outside Buckingham Palace. "Then by special royal proclamation, for one day and one day only, I, Gloria Goddard, announce that you, the members of the Science Inspectors, are entitled to two items of candy for the special sale price of... FREE!"

For a long moment, none of the kids moved or spoke. Gloria Goddard was the type of businesswoman who could make used car salesmen tremble. Meaning, she was tough. Chicago tough. She was not the type of woman who did free. Not ever. And that told Angela everything she needed to know about how grateful Gloria was to be reconciled with Mr. Bannister.

But when that moment ended, several things happened at once. Jamie thrust his fist into the air and screamed like some kind of warrior in a Scottish Highlander movie. Howie turned around, sprinted, and jumped, and who should catch him in midair but his best friend, Norah. "Thank you," Angela said.

All Gloria did was smile and say, "No, dear, thank

you. Now, what will you have?"

Angela picked out something she'd never tried before—a two-foot-long rainbow-sprinkled licorice from Gloria's Luscious Licorice collection. Then she reminded Angela to pick out a second item.

"I'm not sure. Everything looks so good. Have any suggestions?"

"Well, whenever your father comes in, he gets a six-pack of our Crazy Chocolate-Covered Cherries."

"My dad comes in here?"

"Of course he does. Tony's a Brundon Park kid, after all."

"My dad's not a kid."

"He is to me. He was in high school when I started this joint, and I remember when he first started dating your mother. He made sure to bring her into my shop. Of course to show her the greatest candy shop in the world, but I also think he wanted me to meet her. She was very special."

"Yes, she was. Has, um, my dad been in lately?"

"He came in once since you moved back in order to say hello, but not since. I'm sure he's busy helping with the restaurant."

"Then maybe I'll get some of those chocolate-covered cherries to share with him."

She winked. "That's an excellent choice."

Gloria loaded the four friends up with their free candy, then they sat down at one of the two small round tables in the corner of the store.

"Mind if we ask you some questions?" Angela asked.

Gloria clapped her hands together excitedly. "That sounded official. Don't tell me—you kids are in the middle of another investigation."

"We are," Howie said between licks of his Impossibly Large Lollipop. "Someone broke into Mrs. Kopecki's apartment and stole something."

"Poor Karla! What did they steal?"

"Her husband's old watch," Norah said. "But it's also possible they stole something else."

Jamie nodded. "There's some evidence to suggest the thief's main purpose was to steal her secret chocolate chip cookie recipe."

"Really?"

"We know you sponsor the cookie contest at the neighborhood festival," Angela said. "We also know it's coming up soon. We were hoping you might have some insight about the other competitors."

"Especially those competitors who really hated losing to Mrs. Kopecki every year," Jamie clarified.

"Oh! I see where you're going with this. You really

think someone would commit a crime just to win a cookie contest?"

"Honestly," Angela said, thinking about the Missy Price Murder Mysteries that she loved to read, "some people commit crimes for far, far less. So, who comes to mind?"

"Definitely Sofia Pantano."

The kids exchanged a look, which Gloria noticed. "She was already on your radar, wasn't she?"

"Yep. According to Mrs. Kopecki, Sofia's come in second or third every year. Plus, they apparently have never gotten along, but Mrs. Kopecki wouldn't say exactly why."

"That doesn't surprise me. Karla isn't much of a gossip. Thankfully, I am. You want to know the real reason why Sofia hates Karla so much? It's her husband, Glen. He and Karla are old schoolmates. Even went on a few dates back in the day. That alone makes Sofia jealous. The fact that Glen and Karla still get along so well only makes it worse. Sofia's wildly irrational that way. And the fact that she comes up short to Karla every year in the cookie contest? That's just an extra kick in the teeth from Sofia's perspective. If you were looking for someone with a motive to steal Karla's recipe? Someone who also lives in her building? I'd say Sofia is your number-one choice."

"That was our thought as well," Angela said. "Unfortunately, we haven't found any evidence tying her to the crime. Can you think of anyone else who might hold a grudge from the cookie contest?"

Gloria nodded. "Definitely. One other gal. Mind you, she doesn't have personal history with Karla the way Sofia does, but she was plenty angry about Karla winning every year. Plus, there's another reason I'd look into her."

"What's that?"

"Because of her son."

"Who's her son?"

Gloria looked around nervously, which was odd. To Angela, Gloria Goddard wasn't the type of woman who got nervous about much.

But she was definitely nervous. Or more precisely, scared.

"The woman's name is Octavia Kuhl. And her son? Victor. Victor Kuhl."

CHAPTER 8

GOING ROGUE

Norah was the first to speak as they walked away from the candy shop.

"I vote that we end this particular investigation. Remember what Captain Healy told Mrs. Kopecki? That it was probably the work of street thugs? And if that particular thug is Victor Kuhl, we don't want any part of it."

"I have to agree with Norah on this one," Howie said. "As long as it might be old-lady-on-old-lady crime, I was fine with it. But Victor Kuhl? A real criminal? I'm not sure you guys have noticed, but I'm not what you would call tough."

"You don't say," Jamie teased. "The way you ran and jumped into Norah's arms back there, I never would have known."

"Hey," Howie said defensively. "I didn't do that because I was scared. I did that out of pure, unadulterated joy. Had

I been scared, I would have used Norah as a human shield."

"Which he's done on several other occasions, just in case you're curious," Norah said.

"So, you guys are telling me that the only kinds of investigations we can do are the ones that lead to the criminals who aren't scary?" Angela said.

Howie smiled. "Exactly!"

"But that's not realistic," Angela said. "Most crimes are done by real criminals. Not nice old ladies."

"Correct," Norah said. "And most crimes are investigated by real police officers. Not nice little kids. Just to clue you in, Moretti, I have big plans for my life. Most of which include me holding on to that life."

"Meaning?"

"Meaning it's time for me to go do some homework and eat dinner with my family. If you have any more ideas for Operation Green Flannel, I'm game. But I'm retiring from the crime team. Howie too."

"I am?" he said.

Norah narrowed her eyes at him. "Yes, Howie, you are."

His face fell. "Okay."

"But guys, we're the Science Inspectors. I can't do this without you."

"Then don't," Howie said. "Let's just hang out at the lab and do crazy experiments together."

"But..." Angela pleaded. "Mrs. Kopeki's special watch! It meant so much to her. Right, Jamie?"

Jamie sighed. "Maybe they're right, Angela. You're still new to Brundon Park, but we've lived here our whole lives. We've learned how to navigate our neighborhood. How to stay safe. For instance, we never go to the far-eastern end of the neighborhood where Victor and his crew hang out because we know that would be stupendously dumb. If you're serious about helping Mrs. Kopecki, I'll go with you to talk with Captain Healy. I probably get along with him better than you do. We can tell him what we've learned, and then he can take it from there."

"But you saw the way he acted. He doesn't see this as a priority. And when we tell him this was really about a cookie recipe, then he *really* won't take it seriously."

Jamie nodded. "But it's probably the best we can do under the circumstances."

Angela looked at her friends and tried to remind herself about what was important here. That she was still the new kid in a new school in a new town, and she'd already made friends. And yet, she couldn't help but feel incredibly disappointed. She loved mysteries. She was obsessed with how Missy Price used science to help solve mysteries. And the feeling she'd had when they'd solved the case of the old hot rod had been so good. She hated to think all of it was over already. And yet, she understood what her friends were saying. She couldn't force them to do something they thought was dangerous.

So, Angela decided on an approach she'd gotten accustomed to this past year.

She'd just have to figure it out herself.

"I understand, guys. I really do. Why don't we all go home, do our homework, and then chat later about how to move Operation Green Flannel forward tomorrow?"

They walked down Hooper Street together, then Angela said goodbye to her friends. Norah and Jamie kept walking toward their homes. Howie went into his apartment building across the street, and Angela went down the back alley to the entrance she almost always used to enter Moretti's Italian Restaurant. But before she went in, she paused, then walked back out onto the street and turned right. A few minutes later, she arrived and sat on a bench across the street from Mrs. Kopecki's four-story building.

She pulled a notebook out of her blue backpack and looked through her notes.

"Okay, Moretti," she said to herself as she tapped her

pen against the notebook. “What do we know?”

The crime. The crime took place on Tuesday somewhere between 2:30 p.m. and 6:00 p.m. when Mrs. Kopecki was at bridge club down at the VFW, the same as every other Tuesday. There was no sign of forced entry, meaning someone either had the key or was good at picking locks. Her late husband Bobby’s watch was stolen, and though the watch looked nice, it was broken, probably making it worth very little money. But it was of incredible emotional value to Mrs. Kopecki because it reminded her of her husband.

One of the oddities of the crime scene was the discovery of salt on the floor in front of the buffet cabinet. This had led them to the hypothesis that maybe the thief had broken in to steal Mrs. Kopecki’s famous chocolate chip cookie recipe and only took the watch after the fact. Sofia Pantano had emerged as a likely suspect due to her long-term conflict with Mrs. Kopecki and her disappointment at always losing to her in the cookie contest. Talking to Gloria Goddard about the contest led to yet another suspect. A woman named Octavia Kuhl, who was made all the more suspicious because of her son, a neighborhood street thug named Victor Kuhl.

Angela stared at her notes, then tapped her pen

against the notebook again as if she was trying to pull some meaning from the words. Then she thought about Missy Price.

What would she do in this situation?

Simple, Angela thought. Missy Price would find more evidence. She looked at her notes again and noticed something she'd written down—there were no security cameras inside Mrs. Kopecki's building. But then she thought of something Gloria had mentioned—she'd seen Angela enter the store from her security feed. Maybe Mrs. Kopecki's building didn't have cameras inside the building.

Maybe the cameras were on the *outside* of the building.

Angela hustled across the street, where she could examine the building more closely. She started with the steps, then walked slowly along the front of the building looking for any sign of a security camera.

But she found none.

Bummed, she started back across the street where she'd left her backpack on the bench. And that's when she noticed them.

On the electronics repair store across the street were two security cameras. One was positioned to see every person who walked in and out of the store. But the other one was positioned to get a wider view and was pointed directly at Mrs. Kopecki's building.

Bingo.

"What can I do for you?" asked the old man with bushy gray hair as he looked over his newspaper.

"Do you by chance know Mrs. Kopecki from across the street?"

The man put down his newspaper, his eyes now squarely focused on Angela. "Sure I know her. Fixed her television and her vacuum cleaner before. Why do you ask?"

"Because someone broke into her apartment on Tuesday and stole something. I'm helping her figure out who."

"Oh, are you now? And how does this concern me?"

"I noticed one of your security cameras faces her building. I was wondering if you might let me take a look at the footage from the hours that the crime took place. Maybe we'll get lucky and catch the thief on tape."

The old man kept looking at Angela, as if sizing her up.

"This really happen?"

"Sure did."

"And letting you see this footage would help her out?"

"It sure would."

"Fine. Gino!" he yelled.

A young man appeared from somewhere in the back. He was in his early twenties and had dark framed glasses and wild curly black hair.

"I need you to do something for me, and don't argue or ask what it's for. I need you to show this young lady some security footage from Tuesday. Can you do that for me?"

The young man nodded unenthusiastically. "I guess." Then he looked at Angela and sighed. "Come back here with me."

He sat down in front of a computer monitor, then ran the footage back to Tuesday afternoon at 2:15 p.m. Not long after that, Angela could see Mrs. Kopecki leaving her building to go play bridge. Then Gino ran the footage forward. Every once in a while, Angela would tell him to stop and go back, and then she would look until she decided there was nothing to see. When they'd run through all the footage one time, Angela asked if they could do it again. Gino wasn't too happy about it, but Angela gave him the best puppy-dog face she could muster, and he relented. This time, at 4:00 p.m. on the footage, Angela noticed someone she'd glossed over the first time. He was large. Muscular. And even though it had been terribly hot the last few days, he wore gray sweatpants, a gray sweatshirt, and a dark stocking cap. The man stopped at the bottom of the steps of the four-story building, looked around for only a moment, then walked up the stairs and entered the building.

"Could you run that back one more time?" she asked Gino.

The young man flashed her an annoyed expression and asked, "Why?"

"Because this guy looks suspicious."

He eyed her curiously. "You really don't know who that is?"

"No, I don't. I'm new to the neighborhood."

"Allow me to educate you. That right there is a man you do not want to know."

Angela got an odd feeling in her belly.

"Is it Victor Kuhl?"

The young man nodded gravely. "Why exactly are you interested in this footage?"

"Because I'm investigating a crime. And thanks to you, I think I just figured it out."

CHAPTER 9

DESPERATE ESCAPE

Angela thanked Gino and then the old man at the front counter and hurried away. She headed down Hooper Street, wondering if she'd just cracked the case wide open, when suddenly a creepy feeling came over her. As if someone might be following her. She sped up, but the feeling persisted. Finally, she dared to turn around, and she was right. She was definitely being followed.

"Jamie McDermott!" she said. "You about scared me to death. What are you doing?"

He folded his arms. "I think the question is, what are you doing? As in, what were you doing in the electronics store?"

"None of your business," she said defiantly.

"I knew you would do this."

"Do what?"

"I knew you would go off and keep investigating alone. That's what I told Norah, and she agreed. Because you're stubborn like that."

"I am not."

"You are and you know it. So, I thought I'd come back here and make sure you didn't get into any trouble."

"Well, I haven't. So, if it's all right with you, you can go home and let me be."

He looked at her curiously. "You trying to get rid of me?"

"No."

"Because it feels like you're trying to get rid of me."

She said nothing.

"I knew it," he said. "Why don't you tell me what's really going on here?"

"Listen, Jamie. If all you're going to do is tell me to drop the case, I don't really want to tell you anything. But if you're actually interested in helping, I'd consider telling you how I just busted this case wide open."

He narrowed his gaze. "You did?"

She made an explosion gesture with her hands. "Wide open."

He rolled his eyes. "Fine. I'll help you, but only because I don't want to see the new kid in the neighborhood get thrown to the wolves. So, who did it?"

"You promise to help?"

"I promise."

"Do you pinky promise?"

"Angela!"

"Fine. It was Victor Kuhl."

Jamie threw both hands into the air. "Of *course* it was. And let me guess. You're going to go over to Victor's house and arrest him yourself."

"More like, question him."

"Wait, what? You're serious?"

"Like a heart attack."

"You really are stupendously dumb."

"Don't forget stubborn."

"Why can't we just go to the police?" Jamie asked.

"I've been through that already."

"If I don't go with you, then you'll just do this yourself. That about it?"

Angela nodded. "I think that covers it."

"Angela Moretti, if I don't live long enough to drive that old GTO Uncle Nick and I are fixing up, I'm gonna be awfully mad."

"I take it that's a yes."

He shook his head. "Be friends with the new kid, they say. It will be a blast, they say. Fine. I guess we're going to the east side. I know a shortcut."

The buildings on the east side of Brundon Park where Victor Kuhl and his crew lived and hung out were broken down and dilapidated—and if Angela was being honest, a bit scary. She and Jamie hid behind a dumpster. A tough guy, maybe in his early twenties, was hanging out on the sidewalk as if acting as a lookout.

Jamie turned to her. "What's your plan?" he whispered.

"My plan? I don't really have one. Thought I'd wait for some inspiration. A fly-by-the-seat-of-my-pants sort of thing."

Jamie pressed his fingers into his temples and rubbed them. "Deep thoughts, Jamie. Deep thoughts." Then he looked back at Angela. "I mean, do you plan to just ask Victor if he did it?"

"As a matter of fact, I don't. I'm not that stupendously dumb. I just wanted to observe things for a while and get a feel for Victor and his crew. I was hoping we'd notice something that would lead us to the truth."

"What truth?" a man growled.

They spun around to find not one, but two men behind them. Large, well-muscled men, glaring and sneering at Angela and Jamie.

"Whatcha doing?" asked the man on the left.

"Us?" Jamie said. "We're not doing anything."

The man on the right stepped closer. "So, what are you doing *here*?"

"Looking for my retainer!" Angela said. "You know

how expensive those things are. So here we are, looking in the dumpster for a retainer. What a life, right?"

The man grabbed her by the shirt. "You trying to be funny with me?"

"Hey!" Jamie said. "Let her go."

Then the other man clamped onto Jamie's arm. "No, I don't think we will. I don't think we will at all. Because the two of you? You're coming with us."

# # #

They took both Angela and Jamie's cell phones and snatched Angela's backpack as well. Then they threw the kids into a dark closet in the basement of one of those broken-down buildings.

"Wait here and be quiet," the man said. "We need to speak with Victor." Then he slammed the door shut, and Angela heard the lock click.

It was practically pitch black in that closet, and Angela immediately felt claustrophobic. She started freaking out, her heart racing, her breath getting shallower. They had to get out of there. They had to. Angela felt around the walls until she found a switch that brought some light to their situation.

"We're in a maintenance closet," Jamie said.

He was right. There was an old mop and bucket, a

rusty metal shelf filled with bottles of cleaner, a faucet—probably for filling the mop bucket—and a drain in the floor.

"Maybe we could use the mop as a weapon and fight our way out as soon as the door opens?" she asked.

"That would never work," Jamie said. "Victor Kuhl is as tough as they come. Then there's the two guys who brought us in. And who knows how many guys they've got in this place. We need something more than a simple weapon."

Angela looked at the bucket.

"We could fill it up, create a distraction, then run for it and topple the bucket over, making the floor slick enough to wipe a couple of those guys out. At least for a moment. Then maybe, just maybe if we run fast enough, one of us could get outside and flag down some help."

Jamie shook his head. "I don't think that's good enough. We need something better. Bigger."

Angela studied the old bottles of cleaner and wondered what Missy Price might do in this situation. Missy was a forensic scientist, which helped her not only solve crimes, but sometimes get out of impossible jams. Among the bottles of cleaner were two particularly powerful cleaners, ammonia and bleach. And what would Missy Price do with ammonia and bleach?

Answer—absolutely nothing. Missy was a poison expert, and anybody with a rudimentary understanding of chemistry knew that you never, ever mixed ammonia and bleach. Doing so created something called phosgene gas, but most people knew it by another name—mustard gas. Mustard gas had been made famous during World War I and was one of the reasons why it was considered the worst war in history until World War II decided to beat it just two decades later. Mustard gas was deadly. Angela had read about situations where real people had tragically died after accidentally mixing the two common household cleaners together.

And then a crazy thought hit her.

"You know what happens when you mix ammonia and bleach?" she asked Jamie.

"Sure do. That's why you never mix them. Not ever. You shouldn't even store them in the same place like this. Uncle Nick taught me that."

"You're right. Mixing them would be a death sentence, or maybe it could form the basis for a gigantic bluff. The kind of bluff that just might help us escape."

"How do you figure?" Jamie asked.

Angela went over the plan she was forming on the fly. Once she convinced him it was worth a shot, they got to work. Step one was to cover their faces with something, so they both took off their socks, put their shoes back on, and tied the socks around their mouths to help protect them from any fumes. Next step was to pour the ammonia down the drain. For the bluff to work, they needed the illusion that they'd made a terrible mistake, and enough odor to make it seem genuine. Ammonia would provide that odor. Then they partially filled the now-empty ammonia bottle with water. They went over the plan two more times. And finally, they both quietly said a prayer, and Angela hoped beyond hope that somewhere her mom was watching over her.

On the count of three, they began screaming the most hideous and painful-sounding scream either of them could produce and started to pound on the door like maniacs. When the door flew open, both of them coughed and wheezed and staggered out of the closet like crazy zombies. Angela was holding the fake bottle of ammonia as she staggered, and liquid spilled out of it and all over the floor.

"Oh, no!" she screamed. She closed her eyes and kept coughing. "I made a terrible mistake. I mixed the ammonia and the bleach. I think I'm going to die. We're all gonna die if we don't leave!"

Angela opened her eyes just enough to see Victor Kuhl looking around at his crew frantically, not quite sure what to do. Then one of the men ran over to the closet and looked inside. He pulled his head back out and covered his nose. "It smells terrible in there, boss. I think she's telling the truth."

Victor looked at the guy, then back at Angela and Jamie, who continued to cough and scream. Then he started sprinting for the exit. "Everybody, get outta here!"

They ran in one direction while Angela and Jamie went the other, going up a flight of stairs before finding an exit door. They burst out into a small backyard that looked like so many of the other small backyards in Chicago except this one had all the trashy signs of abandonment. They stopped and listened.

"You hear that?" Jamie asked.

Angela nodded. "Sounds like voices somewhere in the front of the house."

They made their way through the backyard and squeezed through a hole in the fence. The alley was spooky. Dusk was coming fast, so things would be getting darker with every minute. They walked down the alley, still not sure of their next move.

Then Angela heard voices and froze. She and Jamie turned around to see a menacing figure at the other end of the alley. It was one of Victor's men, and he pointed at them. "They're in the alley!" he shouted. Then he sprinted for them, and Angela and Jamie had no choice. They ran at top speed, and Angela didn't look back.

At the end of the alley, Jamie turned left and ran toward the street, and she followed. Her legs were tired and she was getting winded, but she didn't dare stop. On the street, a car sped past and though she waved to it, they just kept going. Then she heard a voice erupt. "Get them now!"

She followed Jamie, and that's when she saw another car, this one headed right for them. As far as she knew, this might be one of Victor's cars, but she had to take a chance. She jumped into the street and waved her arms like a crazy person. The car had little choice but to hit the brakes and screech to a halt. Much to her shock, she recognized this car. It was a red Mercury Cougar, and it not only stopped but spun in a half circle, the passenger window already open. The driver screamed, "Get in now, both of you!"

The car door flew open, and they dove inside just as Victor and his men came up behind them. Then the car finished turning around, but instead of flying back down the street, it came to a complete stop. Angela looked at her father. "Dad, what are you doing? We've got to get out of here!"

He shook his head. "No, mia, we don't. You two need to stay here while Victor and I have a little talk."

CHAPTER 10

KUHL AND COMPLICATED

Angela rolled down the window in the back seat. She and Jamie watched as her father walked up and stood four feet away from Victor Kuhl. Victor's hands were in his pockets. Her dad's were at his sides, balled up into fists.

"Why is your dad facing off against Victor Kuhl?" Jamie asked.

Angela was curious about that as well. She had no idea.

Then a most improbable thing happened.

Victor smiled. So did her dad. Then the two of them did that side-hug sort of thing men do from time to time.

"What on earth?" Angela muttered.

"Been a long time, Tony," Victor said.

"Yes, it has. Yes, it has."

"Hey, goes without saying, but I was so sorry to hear about your wife."

"Thanks, Victor. I appreciate it."

"You haven't been by to say hello since you've been back."

Her father shrugged. "Restaurant keeps me pretty busy."

"I get it, I do. You've got a reputation. So do I. I get it."

"Thanks for calling me, Victor. I had no idea Angela was hanging out in this part of the neighborhood."

"My guy gave me her cell phone, and it didn't take me long to figure out this was your kid, so I called you immediately. I was going to get her and her friend when things got a little crazy."

"Crazy how?"

"I would ask your daughter because I think maybe she pulled a fast one on me."

Her dad smiled at that. "Imagine that. A Moretti pulling one over on Victor Kuhl."

Victor smiled as he handed her father a blue backpack and two cell phones. "Okay, wise guy. It was great to see you, really. Now get out of here. I got a reputation to protect."

As her father got into the car, Angela had an idea. Since she was here and since her dad appeared to be on good terms with Victor, this might be her only opportunity.

"Excuse me, Mr. Kuhl," Angela said as politely as she

could. "I have a question for you."

Angela's dad whipped his head back and gave her the look, then shouted out the window. "No, Victor, she doesn't."

Victor smiled as he came toward Angela's window. "Nah, Tony, let the kid ask. She's got gumption. I like gumption."

"Well, the thing is, I was just wondering... why security footage from the electronics repair shop shows you walking into Mrs. Kopecki's building at four p.m. the day that her precious broken watch was stolen."

She heard her dad gasp and start mumbling a prayer, but her eyes stayed on Victor, and his eyes stayed on her. He leaned close to her window and said, "Ain't none of your concern. All you need to know is this. Mrs. Kopecki has always been good to me, and I would never do nothing to her."

"Then who took her watch?" Angela asked.

"Beats me. If it was someone from the streets, I would've heard about it and I would've handled it. Like I said, she's always been good to me."

# # #

When Angela entered Moretti's, Nonna stopped stirring the sauce, got down from her step stool, and came over and gave her a hug. The adrenaline of the whole episode was fading, and Angela felt herself practically collapse into the old woman's arms. When she finally let go, Angela noticed they weren't alone.

Howie and Norah smiled as Angela's father put a hand on her shoulder.

"You appear to have good friends, mia."

Jamie came up alongside Angela. "I texted them a few minutes ago. You guys are quick."

Norah nodded. "When you went back to check on our girl, I decided to do homework at Howie's, so we were just across the street."

"And per the second-best friend contract, I had to make sure you were still in one piece. Everything still in working order?" Howie asked.

"Thankfully, Victor Kuhl is a nice guy," Angela said.

Her father looked down at her. "Let's get one thing straight. Victor is not and never has been a nice guy."

"But you guys talked like you were old friends."

"I've known Victor for a long time, that is true. But we aren't friends."

She nodded as if she understood, though she really didn't. But it was best if she left that alone for now. "Thanks for coming, Dad. I was starting to get scared."

He breathed a big sigh of relief, then suddenly his face

changed. Gone was the loving and caring face of a few moments before, and it was replaced by the typical face her father wore around her. Stern and disappointed.

"This is the part where you explain just what is going on. And you'd better tell me the truth, the whole truth, and nothing but the truth."

So, Angela did. With the help of her friends, she told her dad the entire story about their investigation into Mrs. Kopecki's missing watch. And when she got to the part about checking out the security footage at the electronic repair shop, Norah and Howie were particularly interested.

"She really is stubborn, nosy, and dumb," Jamie remarked.

"Yeah," Howie agreed. "But you gotta hand it to her, she's pretty good at this investigation stuff."

Then Angela told them how she and Jamie were taken to the abandoned building and about her bright idea for escaping.

"Science for the win!" Howie said after she'd explained it all.

"More like poker," Norah said. "That was quite a bluff."

"Well, I'm quite the actress. And should any of you need someone to play the part of damsel in distress from mustard gas exposure, I'm pretty convincing. So, while they ran one direction, we went the other. We were running for our lives when my dad showed up to save our bacon."

"Except Victor was about to let us go," Jamie said as if offering an objection.

"I know," Angela said. "But we didn't know that at the time, and the story's way cooler if people think we escaped all on our own." Then Angela looked at her father sheepishly. "I don't suppose you're going to forget this whole thing ever happened."

"Not on your life. When I received a phone call from Victor Kuhl about my daughter? You scared me tonight, mia. Thankfully, working in an Italian restaurant is an excellent way to pay me back. I'd say another twenty years might just do the trick."

Angela groaned, and her father smiled. Then he left her to be with her friends. They grabbed some spaghetti and meatballs and headed down the hallway to the small room where they sometimes hung out. When Angela finished half her plate, she wiped her mouth and asked her friends the question she'd been dying to ask.

"So, if Victor Kuhl didn't steal that watch, who did?"

In unison, all three of her friends responded by throwing their napkins in her face.

"I'm serious."

"We know you are," Norah said. "Which is why we pummeled you with our napkins."

"Listen, I know tonight was a colossal failure. And yet, we still learned something. We learned Victor Kuhl didn't do this."

"You believe him?" Jamie asked.

"I actually do," Angela replied. "Victor also said he doubted it was someone from the street."

"Which is contrary to Captain Healy's theory," Norah pointed out.

"So, if Captain Healy's wrong and Victor is right, that puts suspicion right back on someone like Sofia Pantano," Angela said.

Howie frowned. "But we don't have any evidence for that."

"Then we need to get some," Angela said excitedly.

Norah, Howie, and Jamie all exchanged weary looks.

"Didn't you learn anything from what happened tonight?" Jamie asked.

"Of course I did. Never mess with someone like Victor Kuhl ever again. But an old lady like Sofia Pantano? That's completely different."

Norah groaned. "You're not going to give up on this, are you?"

"Not on your life."

Norah shook her head. "I was afraid of that. Fine—tomorrow after school, we can keep digging. Let's talk with Edna Henson. She's the busybody of that entire building. I bet that would be a good place to start."

"Perfect. Now, did anybody come up with more ideas for Operation Green Flannel?"

Norah smiled at Howie. "Show her."

"Show me what?"

Howie pulled out his phone, then spun it around. "I give you the website for Operation Green Flannel."

"You made a website? How's a website gonna help us?"

"Just you wait and see. By the way, it's amazing what we can come up with while you're out there trying to get yourself killed," Norah said.

"But one important question first," Jamie said. "What size T-shirt do you wear?"

# # #

Angela found her father sitting on his bed, laptop on his knees, reading glasses perched at the end of his nose.

"I'm not sure I'll ever make sense of these numbers," he said without looking up. "Restaurants aren't what I'd call a high margin business."

"Then why are you doing it?" she asked.

He looked up at her and closed the laptop.

"Listen, mia. I know things have been hard since Mom, and I know that I've been super stressed since coming back to Brundon Park. I'm sorry."

She sat on the edge of the bed with one foot tucked under her. "You don't have to be sorry, Dad. It's just a hard situation all around."

He nodded. "But tonight, when Victor called about you, my mind went to the worst place..." He stopped himself. "Well, that made me realize that I need to enjoy and appreciate what I've still got."

"Dad?"

"Yes?"

"You looked afraid when you came to get me."

"That's because I was," he said.

"You ever gonna tell me the real story about you and Victor?"

He shook his head. "No way. But this is what I'll say. Brundon Park can be a fabulous place to live and grow up, but like lots of Chicago, it can be complicated. When I was young, I sometimes gravitated toward the complicated. And let's just say, Victor was part of that equation. And no, I'm not going to give you any more details. But all that history is part of the reason why your mom and I decided not to raise you here, and why I was hesitant to bring you back when she died."

"But you did."

"Yes, mia. I did. Because despite the Victor Kuhls of the world, Brundon Park is home. And after what happened, I needed all the home I could get. We both did."

Angela threw her arms around her dad's neck and hugged him tight. He hugged her right back. Then she handed him a small decorative box, and his eyes lit up.

"Gloria's Crazy Chocolate-Covered Cherries. How did you know?"

She shrugged. "Let's just say, after what happened today, I figured you needed all the home you can get." Then she grabbed one of the cherries, popped it into her mouth, and smiled a chewy, gooey, chocolatey smile. "We both do."

CHAPTER 11

HONK FOR RUBIES

Jamie reached into his backpack and handed Angela a bright red T-shirt. Angela held it up and read what was written on the front. "'Vote for Rubies. Beveridge Rubies!'"

Norah and Howie were smiling.

"You printed up shirts?" Angela asked.

Jamie nodded. "Aunt Rose has a T-shirt press in her basement. She's got tons of cool and weird stuff down there, most of which she tells me to stay out of. But that T-shirt press sure came in handy." He handed shirts to Norah and Howie, who promptly put them on over their existing outfits, so Angela did the same.

"Why aren't you wearing one of these awful shirts?" she asked Jamie.

"Because I'm wearing a different awful shirt," he replied. He held up a green shirt with white lettering that said, *Support Nina Marcus. Vote for the Green Flannel!*

Angela was so confused.

"It's just like you said, Angela," Norah explained. "Reverse psychology. We lean into what Nina hates—namely you, me, and Howie."

"I wouldn't say she hates me," Howie said.

"Fine. She thinks of you like an annoying bug that needs to be stepped on. Is that better?"

"Much."

"And that's why we need to support Team Ruby with every last ounce of obnoxious effort we can muster," Norah explained. "Trust me, the more we like the nickname, the more Nina's going to hate it."

"Meanwhile, we take the one person here Nina likes," Howie said.

"And I wouldn't say she likes me," Jamie objected.

"Are you kidding me, hotshot?" Howie punched him in the shoulder. "She always looks at you with that big goofy grin."

Howie, of course, was right. Angela had seen it for herself. And yet, thinking about it made her blood boil.

"So, you're the one who's going to support her," Howie said.

"You guys think that will be enough?" Angela asked.

"I'm not sure," Norah said. "So, that's where Howie's website comes in."

# # #

Angela, Norah, and Howie screamed like idiots as the students entered Beveridge that morning.

"Vote Rubies for our school nickname!"

"Go, Beveridge Rubies!"

"Honk for Rubies!"

Once they spotted Nina and her friends, they really poured it on. When their arch nemesis saw what they were doing, she got a particularly horrid look on her face. She put her head down and tried to avoid them, but Angela was not going to let that happen.

"Nina! Oh, Nina!"

Nina stopped and turned toward Angela, fire in her eyes. "What do you want?" she said in short, clipped tones.

"I just wanted to thank you. I know you and I didn't get off to the best start, but like I told you earlier, I love this Rubies nickname, and I support you one hundred percent."

It was clear from the slightly panicked look on Nina's face that she still didn't quite know what to do with this information. So, Angela turned Howie's iPad around and showed a website to Nina. The website Howie had built for this very purpose.

"Did you see what's going on? Rumor is, some teachers started this website in opposition to the Green

Flannel being our next nickname. Apparently, there are sinister and dangerous origins to the name 'Green Flannel,' and I'm glad someone brought it to light."

"What sinister origins?" Nina asked, suddenly curious.

"You can read all about it on this website. It's kind of shocking, actually. I'm not usually a conspiracy nut, but this one kind of fits. Anyway, they're gathering signatures for an online petition to remove Green Flannel from consideration." Angela held out a stylus for Nina. "Would you care to sign? Your support would mean everything. Us Rubies need to stick together. Am I right?"

Nina just stared at her. Then the morning bell rang, and she and her friends turned to head up the front steps of the school. And who should be standing at the top but Jamie McDermott wearing his ridiculous green T-shirt. When Nina read it, her entire face lit up. Then she bounded up the steps, hooked her arm through Jamie's, and together they walked into school.

Angela knew he was just doing this as part of the bigger plan. But still, she didn't like it. Not one bit.

# # #

By the time she was five minutes into science class, Angela's mood had finally improved. Her teacher was the best teacher in the entire school. Jaqueline Dupree was a sophisticated middle-aged woman with a PhD in chemistry who nevertheless did not allow her students to call her "Doctor" because she thought it sounded snooty and pretentious. Nobody knew what she'd done in her previous life, only that she'd gotten into teaching just a few years earlier. Plus, Mrs. Dupree, just like Angela, was a big fan of Dr. Jane McGill's Missy Price Mystery series. In Angela's eyes, the woman was practically perfect.

Angela and her lab partner, Mary, were busy testing the pH of an assortment of liquids when someone shrieked. Angela snapped her head up toward the front of the class.

Norah was on her feet with her arms in the air. Orange juice was leaking off their lab table and onto the floor.

"Why are you such a klutz?" Norah asked.

"I didn't mean to," Howie pleaded. "I don't even remember doing it."

Norah held their lab report worksheet in the air. It was soaked with orange juice. Mrs. Dupree came over and shook her head at Howie.

"I know you didn't mean to, Howie, but we have a zero-tolerance policy. It's your choice. Either you get a zero on the worksheet or you owe me a detention after school. It sounds harsh, but we have to understand the seriousness of lab safety. This time you knocked over orange juice. But next time? Well, we don't want there to be a next time. So, what's your choice?"

Howie folded his arms defiantly. "My choice is... that I refuse."

"I'm sorry," Mrs. Dupree said. "You refuse?"

Uh-oh, Angela thought. *Don't do it, Howie.*

"That's right. I refuse to serve detention, and I will not take a zero for this worksheet. I said I don't remember knocking over the orange juice, so I shouldn't be punished for it."

This was not going to end well.

Mrs. Dupree pointed to the classroom door. "Then you will leave my class immediately and report to the principal's office."

Norah looked on in horror as Howie threw his pencil on the floor, then marched out of the classroom and slammed the door.

"I'm sorry you had to see that," Mrs. Dupree said as she faced the class. "But let's use it as a learning opportunity. Take out a blank piece of paper, then write down everything you just observed about that unfortunate scene."

Mary and Angela exchanged confused looks. They weren't the only ones.

"You heard me, class," Mrs. Dupree said firmly. "Write down everything you just observed. Everything single thing. You have five minutes. Go!"

After five furious minutes of writing, Mrs. Dupree asked the class for their observations. She wrote them down on the whiteboard as a list of data points.

"Now," she said as she paced in front of the classroom. "Does anybody think it's unfair that I sent Howie to the principal's office?"

Everyone in the class looked around, a little hesitant to speak. And though Angela was also reluctant, she felt bad for Howie and wanted to defend her second-best friend. She raised her hand.

"Go ahead, Angela."

"I think it's a little unfair."

"And why do you think so?" Mrs. Dupree asked.

"Because, like you already admitted, it was an accident. Howie didn't mean to knock over the juice."

"So true," she replied. "But that's not really the issue, is it? Did I inform the class of the lab accident zero-tolerance rule at the beginning of the year?"

"Yes," Angela admitted.

"Was Howie aware of it?"

"I think so."

"I think so too," she said. "But instead of taking his consequence, he chose to behave rudely, and I cannot stand for that in my classroom. So, I sent him to the principal's office."

Three different students raised their hands to say they thought the punishment was fair. Then Mrs. Dupree looked around the room. "Does anybody else have anything to say about the fairness or unfairness of what happened to Howie Doohan? Anybody at all?"

She paused and waited. The silence was uncomfortable, but she didn't seem to mind.

Then, in the corner of the room, a small, quiet boy named Landon barely raised his hand.

"Landon? Do you have something to say?"

"Maybe," he said cautiously.

"You don't have to be worried, Landon. As long as you are respectful, you can voice whatever opinion you have."

"Well," he said, "I think it's unfair."

"Even after everything I just pointed out to Angela?"

"Yes," he said.

"And why is that?"

"Because," Landon said while looking around, "Howie didn't knock over the orange juice."

"That's absurd, Landon. Everyone saw the orange juice spilled all over Howie and Norah's lab table and on their lab report."

"Yes, ma'am," Landon agreed.

"Are you saying Norah did it?" Mrs. Dupree asked.

"No, ma'am."

"Then what, Landon, are you saying?"

He pointed at Mrs. Dupree. "I'm saying you did it. You spilled the orange juice."

Mrs. Dupree suddenly and quite unexpectedly started to smile. "Well, well, well. It appears somebody was paying attention."

Then before Angela or anyone else could make sense of what was happening, Mrs. Dupree walked to the door, opened it, and there was Howie, grinning from ear to ear. "Howie," she said, "I do believe you need to take a bow because that performance of yours was magnificent."

Howie sat back down while Mrs. Dupree explained. The incident the class witnessed was actually a demonstration she'd cooked up with Howie. She wanted to teach a special lesson about the critical importance of accurate observations.

"You see, class, sometimes our scientific reasoning is sound and solid, but if it's based on faulty observations, our conclusions will be incorrect, and this will lead us to flawed hypotheses. Landon was correct. My actions toward Howie were unfair because I was the one who knocked over the orange juice, not him. So, going forward, always be very, very careful to make the most accurate observations that you can."

Angela smiled. *Not just the best teacher in the school,* she thought. *Best teacher in the world.*

She was still thinking about it during lunch and didn't notice Norah and Howie come up alongside her as she was grabbing her food.

"Can you believe he kept that whole thing a secret from me?" Norah asked.

"I can't," Angela said. "Gotta hand it to you, Howie—that was really good. You certainly had me fooled."

He laughed. "I apologize to both of you for the subterfuge. But it was really fun."

"But enough about Howie's deception," Norah said. "He and I think it's time for the knock-out punch. We all saw Nina this morning, and she's totally on the ropes. But if this is going to happen by the end of the week, we need her to come over to the dark side now. And by dark side, we mean the green side."

"You're saying I need to make a scene?" Angela said.

"Oh, yeah. Big time. The way only Angela Moretti can," Norah said.

"Am I supposed to be a little insulted by that?"

Howie shrugged. "Probably, but who cares? It's one of your superpowers. So, let 'er rip, buddy."

"You're not coming with me?"

Norah shook his head. "Not a chance. We need to keep our distance in case of shrapnel. Both physical and emotional."

"Some friends you two are."

Howie smiled. "I know, right? We're the best. Now, go get 'er, tiger!"

Angela didn't really feel like doing this at the moment, but she knew her friends would keep hounding her until she did. She needed some motivation. She remembered hearing about something called method acting, where actors would imagine an incident in life that evoked a certain feeling or emotion. Maybe something like that would work, so she pictured Nina arm in arm with Jamie as she bounded happily into school that morning. Anger swelled within her immediately. Motivation? Check.

"Hey there!" Angela said as she approached Nina's table. Perfectly on brand, Nina ignored her, so Angela pressed on, walked right up to her, and leaned in close. "Did you get a chance to sign that petition yet?"

"No," Nina snapped, clearly insulted that Angela

would dare to get that close.

"Well, we really need your support. I'm not sure you're aware of this, but you're the most popular girl in school."

"Of course I'm aware of that." Now she was even more insulted.

"Then you know how much we need you to come out against this horrible Green Flannel nickname." Angela leaned in even closer. "Remember, Nina—Rubies rock. And with your support, we're gonna roll!"

Angela could see the anger in Nina's eyes and the embarrassment on her face. Just the idea that she could have anything in common with a peasant like Angela Moretti was clearly driving Nina nuts. She was on the edge, and she just needed one more little push.

"After the previous disagreements we've had," Angela continued, "I thought this was finally an area where we'd find some unity. And quite frankly, I was hoping we could be pals. I even made up some of these cool Ruby T-shirts for you and your friends."

That was the last straw. Nina slammed both hands against the table, stood up, and pushed Angela in the chest.

"Listen up, Little Italy, and listen up good. You and I will never—and I mean not ever—be anything resembling pals. The fact that you even have the nerve to talk to me is bad enough. But to think that we would have enough in common to be friends? To hang out? You must have some sort of major defect to think that could ever happen. Oh, and for the record, Rubies is a stupid nickname!"

"Stupid nickname?" Angela said with plenty of hand gestures and fake outrage. "Then that makes you pretty stupid since you're the one who came up with it, right, Marcus?"

"You are a filthy liar!" Nina snarled. By now, the entire student body was on their feet and converging on the two girls.

"Liar?" Angela said. She twirled around as if she was now performing for the school. "Do you hear yourself? I think you must be the one with the defect because you are definitely the one who wanted us to be the Rubies in the first place—which I love because it's a great nickname and I totally support you, my close personal friend Nina, and I can't wait for Friday when we officially become the Beveridge Rubies!"

"Stop!" Nina screamed. She pointed her finger at Angela like a lethal weapon. *Oh, man*, Angela thought. This was great. Nina was on the verge of spontaneously combusting. "Stop talking and listen to me. In fact, everyone in this stupid school, listen to me right now. This... *girl* not only has bad hair and no sense of style, but she's delusional. So, let me be clear. Rubies is now and forever will be a grade A loser nickname. And anyone who supports that name is a grade A loser, just like Moretti. So on Friday, if you have any brain at all, you will support me, Nina Marcus. Because I one thousand percent throw my support behind the Green Flannel."

The cafeteria was so quiet, you could hear a pin drop. Then Nina's two friends started chanting slowly. "Green Flannel, Green Flannel, Green Flannel." The chant spread like wildfire, and who was in the middle of it but Nina Marcus, thrusting her arms into the air with all the energy of a middle-aged man at a Bears game.

It was, Angela had to admit, pretty spectacular. And so, to put the finishing touch on this performance that would make even Howie proud, Angela made the decision to leave every last speck of dignity behind. She balled up her fists, stomped the floor like a frustrated three-year-old, and screamed as she stormed out of the cafeteria.

CHAPTER 12

COUNTRY CLUBBING

Angela and her friends were laughing about the lunchroom scene after school that day when a text came in from Mrs. Kopecki. *Angela, I am planning to make cookies again tomorrow in case you and your friends have any updates about your investigation.*

"Now, that is a woman after my own heart," Howie said.

"I think you mean your stomach," Norah said. "But lest you think that I'm completely against the concept, let me be clear. I do not hate eating that woman's cookies."

"I too do not hate her cookies," Jamie said. "I wish she was making them today. I was laughing so hard during Angela's lunchroom performance that I forgot to eat."

Angela looked at the rugged boy skeptically. "You, Jamie McDermott, forgot to eat?"

He smirked. "Seconds. I forgot to eat seconds."

"I sense a pattern between you and Howie when it comes to food," Angela said.

"Yes," Norah said. "They're both pigs."

Angela laughed. "Okay, so we'll visit Mrs. Kopecki and her cookies again tomorrow, but I'd feel so much better if we could give her an update other than getting kidnapped by Victor Kuhl."

"You told us Victor said this crime wasn't committed by somebody on the street. And if it had been, he would know," Norah said. "Question is, can we trust him?"

Angela considered that. "I think so. He and my dad have some kind of history going back to when they were young—and before you ask, no, I don't know what that entails, nor do I ever expect my dad to tell me. Note to self—ask Nonna about my dad's childhood shenanigans. But for some reason, I believe Victor that it wasn't a common street thief who did this."

"Which leads us right back to where we started," Jamie said. "This crime was probably committed by someone who knew Mrs. Kopecki."

"My money's still on Sofia Pantano," Howie said. "The two of them have beef that goes way back, plus Sofia's come up short every year in the cookie contest."

Norah's eyes widened. "And remember what Gloria

said? That Sofia's husband and Mrs. Kopecki get along really well, and that's the main source of Sofia's hatred for her. What if Sofia went to her apartment that day to steal the cookie recipe, but then took the watch just to spite Mrs. Kopecki?"

"Whoa," Jamie said. "That's harsh."

"Super harsh. But Norah's right," Angela said. "It makes sense. Sofia not only gets the recipe, but gets back at her rival by doing what? By taking a piece of Mrs. Kopecki's husband. By taking the watch."

"I think it's high time we speak with Sofia Pantano," Howie said. "And yes, that's the first time in my life I've ever said 'high time.' Wanted to try it out. And guess what—you'll be hearing it from me again."

Norah ignored her goofy friend. "The problem is, according to Mrs. Kopecki, most afternoons Sofia's down at the Happy Holland Country Club with her husband."

"Then why don't we just go down and talk with her there?" Angela asked.

Norah and Howie snickered. Then Norah made a face. "Oh, you're actually serious. Yeah, they don't let people like us into the country club."

"People like us?" Angela asked.

"You know, regular people," Howie said. "You gotta

have money or look like you have money or say sophisticated stuff like 'high time.' Bonus if you smoke expensive cigars and talk about your 401K."

Now it was Jamie's turn to laugh. "Howie's actually not too far off, although he forgot about *The Wall Street Journal*. They're always talking about it, and I happen to know this because I kind of sort of happen to know these people. What I'm saying is, I can probably get you in."

"How?" Norah asked.

"I'm a caddy down there, okay?" Jamie said.

"You, a caddy?" Angela said.

"Yes, me a caddy," Jamie said. "And not because I like golf or country clubs. The pay is good. Plus, Uncle Nick says the connections I'll make with members are great for life. He calls it networking. Someday, when I've got my own shop, I want to specialize in working on and maybe even selling high-performance vehicles. The people at the club are the kind of people who own high-performance vehicles."

"Why, Jamie McDermott, I had no idea," Angela said with a smile.

"Oh, cut it out, guys. I'm not any different than I was before. Now, listen. I can get one person in, but not three. Who's going with me?"

"I will." Angela raised her hand a little too excitedly. "I want to see Sofia's expression when we question her. That should tell us whether or not we're barking up the right tree. I say Norah and Howie go back to the lab. Take another look at the photos and evidence bags from the crime scene. I keep feeling like we're missing something. Maybe you two smarty pants can figure it out."

# # #

Jamie escorted Angela through a gate near the back side of the country club with a small sign that read *Caddy Entrance*. A couple of the caddies saw Jamie and gave him a slight nod, but neither of them paid much attention to Angela. "Wait here. I'll be just a minute."

And he was. Just a minute later, Jamie reappeared but looking very different. Gone was his usual uniform of blue jeans, work boots, and T-shirt. It had been replaced by clean tennis shoes, khaki shorts, and the same sort of yellow polo shirt the other caddies were wearing.

"Hey, preppy," she said.

"Don't start," he replied. "I wouldn't make it ten feet into the club wearing my normal clothes. Now, remember. She plays tennis, and the courts aren't far."

They focused their attention on three older women playing tennis on one of the nearby courts. Two women played on one side, like they were part of a doubles team, while one person played singles on the other side. It worked, but it seemed strange. Jamie had pulled up an image of Sofia Pantano from the club's member directory, but none of these women were her.

When the game was over and the women went to switch sides, Jamie and Angela politely stepped onto the court and got their attention.

"Excuse me, ladies. It was a joy to watch you play," Jamie said, speaking differently than Angela was used to hearing from him. "My friend and I have a question. Do you know where Sofia Pantano is?"

One woman put down her water bottle. "She bailed today. Who wants to know?"

Jamie gestured toward Angela. "This is her niece. She thought Sofia was scheduled to play."

"She was," said another woman. "But she texted me this morning. Said she couldn't make it."

The third woman pressed a towel against her sweaty neck. "It's becoming an annoying habit, if you ask me. Either of you play? We could sure use a fourth."

"Sorry, ma'am," Jamie said. "We don't. By chance, do any of you know where Sofia might be?"

Two of the women shook their heads, but the third, the one who'd been playing singles, had a strange expression on her face. Angela decided to press just a bit.

"Do *you* know?" Angela asked.

The others turned to their friend, who looked like a deer caught in headlights. Then finally she said, "She told me not to tell, okay? But it's really not a big deal."

"I beg to differ," said one of the women. "She keeps leaving us high and dry, and I'd like to find out why."

The other woman lowered her voice. "She doesn't want her husband to know, okay?"

"Doesn't want her husband to know what exactly?" one of the other women asked.

"Fine. Here's what I know. Sofia and Glen come to the club, she walks in, then she walks back out, gets into her car, and takes off. Not every day, but starting a few weeks ago, most days. I don't know where she goes, but she returns a little before Glen gets done with his golf game, and she pretends she was playing tennis the whole time. I told her the secret was safe with me and now I'm telling you, so don't you dare rat her out with Glen. And that goes for you kids as well. Are we clear?"

"Yes, ma'am," Jamie said. "Crystal clear."

As Jamie and Angela walked back toward Brundon

Park, Angela was the first to state the obvious.

"So, our primary suspect sneaks away from the country club almost every day so her husband won't know what she's up to. Which means she not only might have been the one who broke into Mrs. Kopecki's apartment, but it begs another question. What else has she been doing?"

"I say we go talk with a person who prides herself on knowing a little bit about what everyone's up to."

# # #

They found Edna Henson on the bottom floor of her apartment building near the mailboxes. Angela watched as she took the mail out of her box, glanced at it, then put it back inside the box and locked it with her key.

Edna noticed them and must have seen the way Angela was looking at her.

"It's one of the small joys of my day, checking the mail, so sometimes I leave the mail in there just so I can check it again. Are you here to see Karla?"

"Not today," Angela said. "Today we're here to see you."

"Me?" She gestured toward herself. "Whatever for?"

"Because," Jamie said, "you seem like the kind of person who looks out for everyone else."

"I guess I try."

"I think you do more than try. Every building needs good neighbors who look out for the welfare of the others, and I think you do that for the people of this building."

"That's awfully nice of you to say, young man. And I suppose that's right."

"And," Angela said, picking right up where Jamie left off, "we were hoping you'd fill in some blanks for us as we continue to investigate Mrs. Kopecki's missing watch."

"I'm happy to help in whatever capacity I can. As I said before, Edna Henson reporting for duty, sir."

"Great. We have some questions about Sofia Pantano. Mrs. Kopecki told us that the two of them don't necessarily get along the best."

"That's one way of putting it."

"But when we suggested that Sofia might be a suspect, Mrs. Kopecki told us that almost every day, Sofia goes down to the country club with her husband."

"That is correct."

"Except that for the past few weeks, things have changed. Were you aware that most days, Sofia sneaks away from the country club in the afternoon?"

"What goes on between Sofia and her husband's got

nothing to do with me," Edna said.

"But?" Jamie said.

"But... I am aware of that as well."

"Here's our question," Angela said. "Where does Sofia Pantano go?"

Edna sighed. "Are you sure this is important to the investigation?"

"We think so," Jamie said.

"Fine. Sofia's been coming back here. To our building. And to her apartment."

"Why?" Angela pressed. "And why does she want to keep that a secret?"

Edna shifted nervously. "I'd really rather not say."

"Is she alone, or are there other people with her?"

"I'd really rather not say that either."

"Then what can you tell us?"

She leaned in and whispered, "The day Karla's watch was stolen? Sofia was definitely here."

Angela and Jamie exchanged a look.

"One more question, Mrs. Henson. Is Sofia here today?" Angela asked.

"She was, and as near as I could tell, she was alone. But she left thirty minutes ago." Edna zipped her lips shut and pretended to throw away the key. "And that's all I'm going to say about that."

CHAPTER 13

PORTRAIT OF A CRIME

Angela glanced at her phone. "It's 4:45 now. At some point, Sofia will go to the country club, pretend that she's done with tennis, and then return home with her husband. She'll probably be home by early evening. We could always come back tonight and visit her, or hope that she's here tomorrow when we give Mrs. Kopecki an update."

Jamie considered the options. "Or maybe she's only out for a few minutes and we just wait for her and get it over with. I'm anxious to speak with her and try to get some clarity on what's going on."

"We could do some homework to pass the time," Angela suggested.

Jamie frowned. "I hate doing homework."

"Which is probably why you need to do some."

"Can we check in with Norah and Howie?" Jamie asked.

"Says the homework avoider."

He smiled. "Or... says the thorough investigator."

Angela gave in, called Norah, and put it on speaker.

"What have you two misfits learned?" Norah said without even saying hello.

"That Sofia Pantano is a mysterious woman and also very difficult to reach. We're currently staking out the building and waiting for her to come home. Did you two geniuses figure anything out?"

"No, but you did just catch us in the middle of a discussion that you might find interesting."

"About what?" Angela asked.

"About science class today."

"I'm interested," Angela said. "I think you'd call that a good hook."

"What was Mrs. Dupree's big takeaway today?" Howie said.

"Easy," Angela said. "To be really careful about our observations."

"Precisely, because sometimes they're not what we think they are. We might think we've observed something which leads to us asking interesting questions and developing hypotheses. And sometimes we learned that though our questions and hypotheses might be logical and scientific..."

"Our observation was faulty," Angela said.

"Exactly."

"You're saying we made a faulty observation?" Jamie asked.

"Maybe," Norah said. "Here's what we know. Mrs. Kopecki's old watch was stolen. And though valuable to her for sentimental reasons, it wasn't worth any money. At least, according to Mrs. Kopecki."

"That's right. She said the old thing never even worked," Jamie said.

"Which led her to conclude the watch was worthless, and that's the observation she shared with us. So, we ended up focusing most of our investigation on another item that *isn't* worthless."

"Her secret prize-winning chocolate chip cookie recipe," Angela said.

"Which seemed to make sense, what with the cookie contest coming up soon. But what if we were wrong this whole time?"

"About?" Angela asked.

"About that watch," Norah said. "And what if we were wrong because Mrs. Kopecki was wrong? Since she knew the watch best, we trusted her to make a valid observation."

Angela could finally see where this was going. "But

what if she didn't make a valid observation? And what if the watch isn't worthless—what if it's really valuable?"

"That might change some things," Howie said.

"Yes, it might," Norah agreed. "Moretti, here's what I need from you. If Mrs. Kopecki has a picture or knows the name of the maker or has any information about the watch, Howie and I can do some digging and see what we find."

Angela sent a text to Mrs. Kopecki, who responded a few minutes later with two pictures of the watch along with a short description. *Purchased at a garage sale on the south side of Chicago back in 1976. The brand was Singleton.*

Angela was forwarding the photos and the text to Norah when Jamie bumped her in the shoulder and whispered, "Look up."

When Angela did, she saw an older but quite attractive woman walking their way. Italian through and through, Sofia Pantano reminded Angela of some of the relatives in her own family except that Sofia was, as Mrs. Kopecki had perfectly described, a bit extra. Jewelry covered her fingers. Bold makeup covered her face. But she wasn't wearing the tennis outfit Angela had expected. Instead, she wore blue jeans and a long white button-down shirt with paint stains on it. The woman hustled up the sidewalk and toward the front of the building in an obvious hurry, so Angela and Jamie stood up in tandem.

"Mrs. Pantano!" Angela said in a loud, authoritative voice.

That caught Sofia off guard because she flinched and then looked thoroughly confused as she turned their way.

"Excuse me?"

"Ma'am, my name is Angela Moretti, and this is Jamie McDermott."

She squinted at Angela and studied her. "Moretti? As in, the restaurant?"

"One and the same."

"Okay," she said impatiently. "What do you want?"

"Many things, I suppose. But I'm going to guess that you're in a bit of a hurry."

"I am, actually."

"So, I'm just going to cut to the chase. On Tuesday of this week, someone broke into Karla Kopecki's apartment sometime between 2:30 p.m. and 6:00 p.m. and stole an old watch of hers. Question one—did you do that?"

The woman's face twisted and contorted in exactly the sort of way you'd expect from someone who was not guilty.

"Are you out of your mind?" she said angrily.

"So, it wasn't you?" Jamie pressed.

"Of course not," she said.

"Then we have just one follow-up question," Angela said. "Do you have an alibi for that time period? And before you say you were at the club playing tennis all afternoon, we know that's not true."

This question landed differently than the first. Sofia's face didn't contort or twist. Rather, her eyes darted around, and her face turned colors. This, Angela knew, was the look of someone who was guilty. Guilty of what exactly, she didn't know.

The woman leaned in and lowered her voice. "As to the alibi, the answer is yes, but it's more complicated than that. And if we could take this inside, I'll try to explain."

They followed Sofia Pantano up to the fourth floor and then into Apartment 47. She set her purse and keys on her kitchen counter, then turned and faced them.

"Why don't you start by telling me what business this is of yours?" she asked.

Angela shrugged. "Captain Healy didn't seem very interested in devoting police resources to helping solve Mrs. Kopecki's case."

"So, we offered our assistance," Jamie said.

"But you're just a couple of kids."

"There's two more of us, actually," Jamie said. "We call ourselves the Science Inspectors. We use science and detective skills to solve cases. And Angela here is our leader." He looked at her. "She's really good at this kind of thing, so when she thinks she can solve a mystery, I believe her."

Angela smiled. It felt good to hear him say that.

"And your expertise has led you to suspect me of stealing that old watch," Sofia said indignantly.

"It did until I saw the expression on your face when I asked you the question. Now I know it wasn't you," Angela said.

Sofia seemed exasperated. "But you want my alibi nonetheless?"

"That's how it works, Mrs. Pantano. You give us a credible alibi, and then we can move on. And just in case you speak with the ladies from the club sometime this week, we may have told them I was your niece."

She threw both hands in the air. "You went down to the club?"

"To speak with you, yes. But don't worry—we didn't talk to your husband, and whatever your secret is, it's safe with us."

She put her head down and shook it back and forth.

"I am so, so dumb. Why didn't I just tell him from the very beginning?"

"Tell him what?" Angela asked.

Sofia sighed. "Follow me."

Angela followed Jamie, who followed Sofia through the living room, down the hall, and then into a bedroom. A small bed was pressed up against one wall. But near the other wall, a canvas tarp lay on the floor. An easel sat on the tarp, and a large canvas painting sat on the easel. It was a portrait. Of a man. An intimidating man Angela recognized at once.

"That's Victor Kuhl!" Angela said, pointing at the canvas.

"And this is where that alibi gets complicated."

"I am so completely confused," Jamie said.

"So am I," Angela added.

Sofia Pantano ran her hand through her hair. "I am too. I can understand why you and Karla suspected me—she and I never got along. Not ever. And yes, the fact that she and my husband used to date was probably the main reason. And then throw in that they still like each other's company? It makes it even worse. I mean, even when her Bobby was alive, the two of them loved to share jokes and memories from the old days. It probably bugged Bobby as much as it bugged me. And then every year, she'd beat me at that stupid cookie contest. I'm Italian, for the love of Pete. Food is in my blood, but I couldn't beat the woman making a simple cookie? Well, the anger and envy ate me up inside. And a couple months ago, when I knew the contest was coming up, I had a realization I wish I'd had years ago. Why was I killing myself trying to be better than Karla Kopecki? Trying to be like her? Why didn't I spend my energy trying to be more like *me*?"

"So, what did you do?" Jamie asked.

"I've always wanted to paint," she said with a sudden twinkle in her eye. "I brought it up with Glen one time way back when, but he laughed. The kind of laugh that makes you feel bad inside. He said it was silly to take up something new at my age. He actually said that. 'My age.' That burned me to no end. And one day I was at the club, and I'd just had it. Enough. So, I stormed off the tennis court. I drove to the art store, bought some supplies, came back here, and started to paint. And wouldn't you know it? I was actually pretty good."

Angela studied the portrait of Victor Kuhl. It was pretty good. *Nope*, she thought. She was no expert, but this was more than pretty good. "This is fantastic."

Sofia smiled. "It is, isn't it? What can I say? The moment I started painting, I knew it was my thing. What a blessing at my age to finally find my thing. So now, whenever I get a chance, I paint."

"And the only time you get a chance is when your husband's out of the apartment golfing," Jamie said.

"Exactly. A huge part of me is afraid to tell Glen about all this. And yes, in case you're wondering, I do clean it up and hide everything before we get home from the club. But I'm afraid that he'll call it silly again or won't think it's good, or worst of all... I'm afraid he won't support me. I just wanted to have this be mine for a little while longer."

"I get it, Mrs. Pantano, I really do," Angela said. "But what I don't get is how you came to paint a portrait of Victor Kuhl."

Her eyes widened as if she understood the oddity of it all. "It's the craziest thing. I showed some of my stuff to the manager down at Nerinx, the neighborhood art store. She said I was a natural. She used the word 'amazing.' She'd never seen anybody pick up painting that fast. Not ever. Then a deep voice asked if I could paint him. I turned around to find an extremely large man standing there. We talked, and I explained I didn't really do portraits. Then he said he had to have it. He was giving it to a special someone. And then he told me how much he'd pay."

"How much?"

"An amount that convinced me that maybe I *do* do that sort of thing."

"And so on Tuesday, when Mrs. Kopecki's watch was stolen?" Angela asked, trying to get back to the issue of the alibi.

"I was in my apartment painting a portrait of Victor Kuhl. He can confirm that if it's necessary."

Angela thought about the security footage from the electronics store across the street. The footage that showed Victor entering that building on Tuesday around 4 p.m.

"Don't worry, Mrs. Pantano. He already did."

CHAPTER 14

A HARDWARE ISSUE

Angela punched the code into the keypad, and the trash chute slid open. She grabbed the bar above her, kicked up her legs, let go, and yelled "Whoopee!", which is what she always did when she used the secret slide entrance into Howie's ground-floor lab.

Jamie followed her, and after they landed in the large beanbag at the bottom of the slide, Angela smelled something, which wasn't unusual in the lab. The difference was, this actually smelled good.

"Did someone make popcorn?"

Norah appeared with a large bowl overflowing with delicious-smelling buttery goodness. "Someone did. And why, do you ask? Because Howie and I did some research and now we have a little movie to show you."

Norah set the bowl on one of the lab tables while Howie started a video on the large computer monitor that was attached to the wall. Angela tossed a handful of popcorn into her mouth while she watched. A familiar theme song played, followed by title graphics suddenly appearing on the screen.

"Hey," Jamie said. "I know this show."

"I do too," Angela said. "*Old Things, Big Prices*. Why are we watching this?"

Norah and Howie exchanged a smile. "Just wait," Howie said. "Just you wait."

An old woman appeared on the left, and one of the stars, a man named Peter Matthewson, appeared on the right. Peter wore round spectacles and a red bow tie. He was the show's antiques expert. The old woman explained how she'd been going through her attic getting ready for a garage sale when she found something that piqued her interest.

An old watch.

Angela leaned forward. "A watch!"

"And not just any old watch," Norah said.

The man examined it carefully and then explained that it was a Singleton, a well-crafted and rare brand from back in the 1940s and 50s. He said there were very few left in the world and that this particular style was probably worth something close to fifty thousand dollars.

"What?" Angela and Jamie shouted at the same time.

Then Howie paused the show, and the four of them looked at each other.

"Mrs. Kopecki's watch is a Singleton," Angela finally said, still in shock.

"Thank you, Captain Obvious," Norah replied. "Thus the reason we showed you that clip."

"Are we saying that her watch, a watch that she thought was worthless, might actually be worth fifty thousand dollars?" Jamie asked.

"We have no idea," Howie said. "We know the watch is broken, so it would have to get fixed. But that might only cost a couple hundred bucks."

"And from the picture you sent me," Norah said, "the watch appears to be in really good condition other than that. So, I don't know if it's worth that much money, but I'm guessing it's worth quite a bit."

"Then this was never about her award-winning recipe," Angela said, still processing it.

"With a watch worth that kind of money?" Jamie said. "I don't think so."

Angela started pacing around the room, talking excitedly. "Then this changes our list of possible suspects. If it was about the recipe, we'd look at other women, especially those who kept losing in the cookie contest. But now... now that it's about the watch, it could be anyone."

"Not anyone," Norah said. "Remember that Victor Kuhl said it wasn't someone from the street. So, it's not a professional thief."

"And not Sofia Pantano," Jamie said. "We had a very enlightening chat with her. Suffice it to say, she's no longer a suspect."

"And speaking of Victor Kuhl," Angela continued, "he isn't either. And yes, I know that's confusing, and we'll explain everything later. Trust me." Then she stopped. "But I don't get it. How could this not have something to do with the recipe?"

"What do you mean?" Howie asked.

Angela walked over to the lab table that held the bags of evidence from the crime scene. Then she grabbed the one containing a white powdery substance. "What about the salt?"

The rest of the Science Inspectors stared at the bag. And by the looks on their faces, they were all curious about where this was going.

"We found salt at the crime scene," Angela said. "On the floor in front of the buffet cabinet where the watch was taken. With the recipe hypothesis, everything fits. Someone stole the recipe out of the salt jar, then noticed the fancy-looking watch and spilled salt on the floor. But if none of that is true... If this was never about the recipe... If this was always about the watch... what explains the salt?"

Howie was about to say something, then stopped. They all looked at each other. Nobody said anything because nobody knew what to say until Norah finally spoke up.

"Maybe the salt didn't mean anything. Maybe it was one of those random freak things. A piece of evidence that wasn't really evidence at all—remember Mrs. Dupree's lesson today about our observations? Mrs. Kopecki was wrong about the watch. It did end up being worth something. Quite a bit, actually. Maybe she was wrong about the salt. Maybe she spilled it when she was baking or cooking, and she just doesn't remember. And therefore, the salt doesn't mean anything."

Angela considered that, then nodded as she kept walking. All of a sudden, she stopped. Her face lit up, and her eyes grew bigger.

"Mrs. Dupree's lesson. We have to be very careful about our observations!"

Norah folded her arms. "That's what I just said. Sometimes I think you really are a misfit."

But Angela ignored her. "We observed salt. On the floor. And we assumed it got spilled."

"Of course we did," Howie said.

Angela got all excited again. "And that observation took us down a particular path because we assumed the only way salt gets on the floor is if it's spilled."

Jamie looked at her curiously. "Where is this headed?"

A big grin spread across her face. "I think... in the direction of the hardware store. Come on, Jamie!"

Fifteen minutes later, Angela and Jamie landed back in the laboratory. But this time, they didn't come empty handed. Angela set a large jug on the lab table. It was filled with a white substance.

Howie shot her a look. "Is that ice melt?"

"That's what a lot of people call it. But did you know that the most popular substance used to melt ice in the winter is nothing other than good old-fashioned sodium chloride?" Angela smiled. "Or known more commonly as... salt."

CHAPTER 15

A REPUTATION TO PROTECT

Norah pointed at the jug. "Road salt!"

"Exactly," Angela said.

"Regular old salt mixes with the water in the ice to become salt water, which freezes at a lower point than regular water," Jamie said. "And this makes the roads less slippery for cars. Or the sidewalks less icy for people."

"And during the winter, they spread this stuff everywhere," Angela said with a sweeping gesture. "I asked the question, how could salt get on the carpet? We assumed it had to be spilled, but that was wrong. During the winter, salt gets spilled all the time by being tracked inside on our shoes!"

"Okay," Howie said, "I get what you're saying. There's just one problem. It's not winter. In fact, this has been the hottest October on record. They haven't begun to spread salt on the roads and sidewalks yet."

"You're right," Angela said. "They haven't. At least, not in Chicago. It's warm here. But," she said with a wide grin, "it's not warm everywhere. In fact, there's at least one place in America where it's cold, right?"

Jamie snapped his fingers. "That's right. I told you about the headline—there was a big snowstorm out east somewhere. Broke the record for the earliest snowstorm in that city's history."

"Any idea which city?" Angela asked.

Norah reached for her phone, but Howie was faster. "Okay, according to the Google thing-a-ma-doodle, it was in... Buffalo, New York!"

Angela and Jamie exchanged a smile. "And do we know of anybody who's been in Buffalo, New York, lately?"

Howie pointed at Norah. "The guy from Big Lou's wearing the royal blue Buffalo Bills shirt. What was his name again?"

"Sid!" Norah shouted. "Sid Granger."

"That's right, ladies and gentlemen," Angela said confidently. "Sid Granger. Sid Granger had just gotten into Chicago from Buffalo where he and his mom, Alma, live. Alma Granger is best friends with none other than Karla Kopecki. When Sid is in town, he visits Karla on behalf of his mom. Even brings her a slice of Big Lou's. And what do you think are the odds that Sid knows all about that watch?"

"I'd say close to a million percent," Howie said.

"And I'm going to guess that one night, Sid Granger was watching an episode of *Old Things, Big Prices* and saw a watch that looked just like Mrs. Kopecki's. He got greedy and he made a plan—to come into town and slip into her apartment while she was playing bridge, then go for pizza and act awfully shocked when he received the call. Then stand by her side while Captain Healy did his five-minute investigation, all the while knowing he had pulled off an incredible little heist. One that might just be worth fifty thousand dollars."

"That's it," Howie said, pointing emphatically at nothing in particular. "That has to be it."

"There's just one problem," Norah said. "How exactly do we go about proving it?"

"I'm not sure we can," Angela confessed.

"Then what do we do?" Howie asked.

"We could go to Captain Healy and tell him what we know," Jamie said.

Angela nodded. "We could. We most definitely could. But I think I have another idea."

She pulled out her phone, called Big Lou's, and asked

for the man himself. “Hey, Lou, Angela Moretti. I’m calling on behalf of Mrs. Kopecki. Her phone went down and she’s trying to reach Sid Granger before he leaves town. Any idea how to get ahold of him?”

“He’s having a slice of pie and a root beer at my counter, so yeah, I got a pretty good idea,” Big Lou said.

“Great,” Angela said, amazed by the good fortune. “Don’t tell him Karla’s looking for him. She’s got a nice surprise for him. We’ll be down there in a few minutes.” She disconnected, then made another call. “Hey, Dad. Yeah, I’m fine. And no, I haven’t been kidnapped. But speaking of that, remember how you and Victor go way back? And remember how you said he thinks Mrs. Kopecki is a real nice lady? Well, I’ve got an idea, but I’m going to need your help. When? Soon. And by soon, I mean right now.”

# # #

Angela climbed onto the stool right next to Sid Granger while Jamie slid into the stool on the other side. Howie and Norah stood behind him.

“Hey, Sid,” Angela said.

He looked at her curiously, then took a sip of his root beer and looked at Jamie to his left.

“Do I know you?” he asked.

"We're friends of Mrs. Kopecki's. We met here the other day, remember?"

"Oh, yeah. Well, that's just great."

Angela smiled and stared at him, and this clearly made Sid uncomfortable.

"Is there something I can do for you?" he asked while grabbing another slice of his pizza.

"I guess you could answer a question. It's simple, really. Why didn't you get rid of the road salt from your boots before you broke into Mrs. Kopecki's apartment to steal her watch?"

Everything about Sid stopped. His hand stopped lifting pizza to his mouth. His face stopped moving. Angela thought his breathing might have even stopped. This was the reaction of a man who had just been caught.

The question was, what would he do next?

When his breathing started again, his eyes narrowed, and his color changed. "That's quite a story you've got there, kid."

"Oh, come on, Sid," Jamie said. "There's no reason to be bashful. If you're going to steal from an old defenseless lady, at least be man enough to admit it."

"Or," Angela said, "if you're not man enough to admit it, maybe you'd be man enough to continue this conversation with me and my friends outside."

Jamie grinned. "We love having conversations outside."

That caught him off guard, and it had the intended effect. He smirked. He smirked a very cocky smirk. Sid Granger was a big guy, and there was nothing about four seventh-grade kids that could possibly intimidate him.

He stood up, laid a tip down on the counter, and said, "I'm happy to continue this conversation outside." He pushed past Howie and Norah, and the four friends followed him out to the parking lot and the unusually hot October night. As soon as he got out there, Sid spun around, eyes hot with rage, teeth snarling. He looked like he was going to kill the Science Inspectors.

There was just one tiny problem.

The Science Inspectors weren't alone.

Tony Moretti emerged from the shadows near the door. And when Sid saw him, his expression changed.

"Hey, what is this?" he barked at Angela's father.

But Tony didn't answer. The answer came from a loud and thunderous voice from behind Sid Granger.

"I think they call it an intervention."

Sid spun around to see the enormous figure of Victor Kuhl. Four scary dudes were behind him, and Sid Granger started to shake.

After that, things went pretty smoothly. They went smoothly because Victor explained how this was going to go, and Sid listened. Victor and his men would escort Sid to wherever he had stashed the watch. Then Victor would give it to the Science Inspectors, who would return the watch to its rightful owner. Everyone agreed that the true identity of the thief would never be revealed because it would break Mrs. Kopecki's heart, and Victor Kuhl didn't want that to happen. Once the watch was restored, that was it. That is, except for one last item. Sid Granger would never, ever show his face in Brundon Park again.

One hour later, Victor met Angela and her friends in front of Mrs. Kopecki's building and handed Angela the watch.

"You're not so bad for an enormous scary guy," she said.

"I know," he said. Then he leaned over and whispered, "Just don't tell anyone. I got me a reputation to protect."

Then Angela and her friends knocked on the door to Apartment 23 and made an old woman deliriously happy.

"But how did you figure it out?" Mrs. Kopecki said as she cradled the old watch lovingly in her hands and fought back the tears that formed in the corners of her eyes.

"Well," Angela said carefully, "I think you'd say we have a pretty 'cool' neighborhood."

Norah rolled her eyes at the pun, but Angela pressed on. "And a concerned citizen came forward after finding the watch."

"That's it?" Mrs. Kopecki said.

"You have that special memory of your husband back. Isn't that what matters the most?" Angela said.

The dam broke for Mrs. Kopecki, and tears flooded down her cheeks. But there was something else. "We did discover one thing during our investigation that I think you ought to know. That watch of yours might be worth a lot of money."

"This old thing?" she said skeptically. "No way. It doesn't even work."

"But suppose it did," Norah said. "It might just be worth fifty thousand dollars."

Mrs. Kopecki's mouth fell open. "F-fifty thousand? How is that even possible?"

"Well, it is," Norah said. "Believe us that it is. Which means, you might want to sell it one of these days."

"Are you crazy? Sell a piece of my Bobby? Never."

"That's what I thought," Angela said. "Then at least do yourself a favor and keep it in a safe."

"How can I ever repay you children?"

"No need," Jamie said. "We don't take money for this. It's just what we do."

Mrs. Kopecki's eyes brightened. "Then would you at least take some more cookies?"

Angela and the others exchanged a look that could best be described as hungry.

"We could probably accept some cookies," Howie said.

"Then it's settled. I promise to bake you dear children my delicious chocolate chip cookies every single week... for the rest of your lives."

CHAPTER 16

FINALLY HOME

On Friday afternoon, the students of Beveridge Middle School assembled to vote for their new nickname. To push their objective past the finish line, Angela and her friends pulled out all the stops. They held up signs that read *Up with Rubies, Down with Flannel.* They wore their obnoxious *Rubies Rock*! T-shirts. Angela even gave an impassioned speech to the school in defense of Rubies and warning of the toxic impact Green Flannel could have not only on Beveridge, but on the entire world for many generations to come.

All the while, Jamie walked around with Nina leading the student body in "Vote for Flannel" chants and then booed Angela mercilessly during her speech. Jamie even built a cool new T-shirt cannon for the day and launched green flannels purchased by Nina's father all throughout the gym. When the final vote was taken, Angela had led the Rubies to less than 10% of the vote. It was a stunning victory for the Green Flannel.

As they left the school that day, Nina and her friends taunted Angela and her friends so mercilessly that Angela just couldn't take it anymore. She stopped and spun around.

"Don't do it, Moretti," Norah warned.

"Don't worry. I've got this," Angela replied.

"We don't believe that," Norah said. "Do we, Howie?"

"Not even for a second."

"Then prepare to be surprised." Angela walked up to Nina and extended her hand. "Just wanted to congratulate you on a great victory."

Nina looked at Angela's hand like it was infected and responded by folding her arms.

"I just really wanted us to be the Rubies. I was clearly wrong."

"Clearly," Nina said.

"And now, Beveridge gets to be the home of the Green Flannel. I mean, Nina, you've been advocating for us to be the Green Flannel for years now, haven't you?"

Nina was about to say something, then stopped because she clearly didn't know what to say.

"Huh," Angela continued. "That's actually not what happened at all, is it? No, what happened is that you wanted us to be the Rubies and then all of a sudden, a few days ago, you decided we should be the Green Flannel. The question is, why? Why did you suddenly change your mind?"

The wheels were turning in Nina's head now. The way her eyes were darting back and forth, the wheels were most definitely turning.

"I mean, it's not like somebody else brought up the Green Flannel to you, is it? Because a girl as pretty and popular and strong as Nina Marcus couldn't possibly be manipulated like that, could she?"

Nina's face did that thing where people are doing mental math, and her face instantly changed. She was starting to understand.

Angela didn't need to see Nina hurt or publicly humiliated or anything like that. Her face, right in that instant, was enough. There was just one more thing to say.

"Gotcha!"

Then Angela walked back to her friends. Jamie had joined them now, and Angela wondered what look Nina had on her face as she realized Jamie wasn't on her team. But Angela didn't bother looking back. Nope, together she and her friends just walked away. And as they did, Angela, Norah, and Howie ripped off their red shirts to reveal their preferred costume for that moment.

Green flannel. Just like Jamie.

"And why?" Norah said to a smiling Howie.

"Because we're the Science Inspectors and..." He laughed maniacally and all four friends shouted in unison,

"THERE'S A SCIENTIFIC METHOD TO OUR MADNESS!"

# # #

Solving the case of the broken watch had been great. Somehow, getting one over on Nina Marcus had been even better. And yet, as good as both outcomes had been, something was still bothering Angela. It bothered her when she went to bed that night, and the next morning, while she helped Nonna in Moretti's kitchen, she kept thinking about it. Like a pebble in her shoe, she just couldn't shake it. There was one last detail in Mrs. Kopecki's case that didn't make sense.

The salt.

And not the salt on the floor. That had already been explained.

The salt on the kitchen counter.

Mrs. Kopecki was clear. In addition to being fastidious about closing her apartment door, she was also fastidious about keeping her kitchen immaculate.

And someone like that does not leave salt on the counter.

So, how on earth did it get there? Because it wasn't Sid Granger.

The longer Angela thought about it, the more she turned it over in her head, the more she became convinced. There really was only one answer.

After the lunch rush that day, she headed down to Mrs. Kopecki's building, walked up to the third floor, and knocked on Edna Henson's door. Ten seconds later, the door opened. Edna looked surprised to see her.

"Hello?" she said as if struggling to remember the name.

"Angela. My name is Angela."

The old woman nodded. "That's right. Well, Angela, what can I do for you?"

"I was just curious how they tasted."

Edna squinted at her through her red-framed glasses. "Tasted? I'm not sure I follow."

"Were they as good as when Mrs. Kopecki makes them?"

Edna's face was still a blank, so Angela persisted.

"I'm talking about the cookies, Mrs. Henson. Mrs. Kopecki's famous prize-winning chocolate chip cookies. I mean, that is the whole reason you stole her recipe, isn't it?"

The old woman couldn't help herself. She instinctively put her hand to her mouth and gasped. She stared at Angela and trembled, fumbling around for what to say. And then finally, "B-but how?"

"How did I figure it out?" Angela asked. "It was several things, really. And when you add them up, I concluded it just had to be you. Take the salt on Mrs. Kopecki's counter. That was a dead giveaway that someone got into her salt container where the secret recipe had been hidden. And then the fact that I already figured out who stole her watch. And no, I'm not telling you. Newsflash—the watch thief didn't leave salt on the counter, but I'm guessing they did accidentally leave the door open. And this, of course, is where you enter the picture.

"Remember, you are Edna Henson reporting for duty, sir. And you keep an eye on things. You told us yourself, 'Karla Kopecki is fastidious about keeping her door shut.' And so, when you were keeping an eye on things, you noticed her door was open, didn't you? And that's when you knew something was up, so you went into the apartment. But Karla wasn't there. Not anywhere. You checked the time. You knew she was at bridge, and you realized your opportunity. To find that secret recipe, the one Karla would never share with anybody. Not even you. And the amazing thing is, you did. You found it."

"W-what are you going to do?" she asked fearfully.

"Me?" Angela said. "I'm not going to do anything. But you? You are going to delete the picture you took of that recipe. And if you wrote it down, you're going to rip it up and burn it. And if you remember it? You're going to do everything in your power to forget it. As long as you do those things, Karla never has to know, and you and I will never speak about this again."

Edna Henson nodded ever so slowly.

Angela walked out of the building. She was finally satisfied, the mental pebble gone. The last part of the mystery solved. She inhaled a deep breath and took all of it in. The heat of the last week had vanished, replaced by cool and crisp autumn air. The trees were changing into a vibrant display of oranges, yellows, and reds. She thought about the good friends she had made. Then she smiled. Turned out, Brundon Park was a pretty nice place to live. And after the hardest year of her life, Angela Moretti was finally home.

THE END

About the author:

Daniel Kenney

Daniel Kenney and his wife live in Nebraska with their eight children and one very tiny dog.

Daniel brings his experience as a high school teacher and a father to the work he does as a children's author.

He has published more than thirty-five children's books and strives to write fun and adventurous stories that affirm timeless values such as courage, friendship, and family.

Chapter Books

For ages 8 to 12

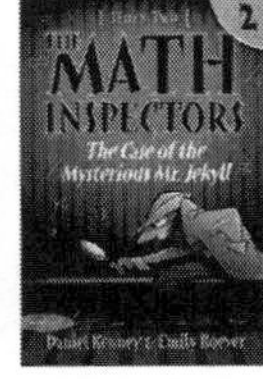

Picture Books

Find his work by visiting:

www.authordanielkenney.com

www.bakkenbooks.com

www.bakkenbooks.com

The mission of Bakken Books is to provide kids with wholesome books that teach character lessons, core virtues, and strong moral values.

We strive to provide content parents can TRUST and kids will LOVE!